TIP THE SCALES

Road Trip romance

A.K. EVANS

Cover Artist
cover artwork © Sarah Hansen, Okay Creations
www.okaycreations.com

Editing & Proofreading
Ellie McLove, My Brother's Editor
www.grayinkonline.com

Formatting
Stacey Blake at Champagne Book Design
www.champagnebookdesign.com

As is the case with any new series, this one is for the loves of my life: my husband and my two boys.
I love you.

TIP THE SCALES

CHAPTER 1

Eleanor

PANDEMONIUM.

Disorder and confusion.

I'd seen it before. But never like I did today.

The worried looks from elderly couples as they walked through the droves of people. The panicked mothers pushing their young children around in shopping carts. Even the men had grave looks of fear plastered on their faces.

It surprised me. Probably more than it should have.

Perhaps I should have heeded the warning signs smacking me right in the face. But I really couldn't imagine it was going to be that bad.

I didn't think I was being naïve. I mean, I grew up in southeast Florida. Hurricanes had become commonplace in my life. I knew the panic nature's fury brought with it. People had the potential to lose their homes when a hurricane hit, so I always felt the fear was justified.

Three months ago, I left Florida. I was seeking

solace from the constant buzz of activity that surrounded me living in West Palm Beach. I was a stone's throw away from Miami, so it felt like no matter where I went, it was always bustling.

Being the introvert that I am, I sought out a place that would give me what I needed. Ultimately, I decided that a little town in northern Maine would provide me the peace and quiet I was so desperately seeking.

It's not that I don't like people. I do. I just couldn't get used to the sheer volume of individuals that were everywhere I went. And outside of my very small circle of friends and family, I found it virtually impossible to meet anyone and strike up new friendships.

When I arrived in White Pine, a quaint little town in Northern Maine, last October, I took full advantage of having the quiet surround me. I bought a beautiful home on a large piece of land and instantly knew I'd never want to leave.

So I didn't.

Literally.

Other than the bi-weekly trip to the grocery store, I rarely went out. Of course, I had no plans for it to always be that way.

The moment spring hit and the weather warmed up, I had every intention of getting out to go exploring.

I wanted to head south so I could see Maine's coastal towns and the lighthouses.

Eastport was high up on my list of places to visit because I wanted to witness the country's first rays of morning sunshine.

I planned to hike in Acadia National Park and on Mount Katahdin.

And I wanted to eat lobster. Lots of lobster.

But I had time. I didn't need to do everything all at once. What I needed for the first few months after arriving in Maine was solace. The rest would eventually come, and I'd be able to appreciate it much more after I'd given myself the time I needed to recharge first.

Right now, though, I was mildly concerned about what I'd just witnessed. Either I hadn't been getting out enough to realize White Pine residents were just like those in West Palm Beach, or something else much bigger than I had expected was happening.

I was in my car on my way home from the grocery store. It was my normal day to shop. Unfortunately for me, there were reports of a winter storm approaching. I guess it was expected that the crowds would be larger than usual considering the impending threat, but what I witnessed was just plain insanity.

And it was alarming.

Because no matter if the individual was old or young, man or woman, they all had one thing in common.

Terror.

I found it concerning mostly because I simply didn't understand why residents of a community that frequently got snow looked that way. It was as though they all feared they were about to experience a once-in-a-lifetime event.

On that thought, I figured it was probably best for me to get online when I got home and check out the weather reports. Maybe I'd missed something and overlooked just how severe the storm was expected to be.

A few minutes later, I turned off the road into my driveway. I stopped at the end to get out and retrieve my mail.

The moment I closed the door on the mailbox, I heard a familiar voice call out to me. "Did you get yourself all stocked up, Eleanor?"

I turned around and saw Walter standing there at the end of his driveway across the street from mine, holding his mail in his hands.

Walt was one half of the elderly, but still spunky, couple that greeted me the day I moved in. His wife, Betty, was the other.

I adored them.

And I instantly warmed hearing Walt call me Eleanor. Of course, it was my name. But nobody really called me Eleanor. It was either Ella, in the case of my friends, or Nora, in the case of my family. I explained this months ago when I moved in, but Walt insisted on Eleanor.

"What's wrong with Eleanor?" he asked when he and Betty had me over for dinner two weeks after I'd arrived in town.

"There's nothing wrong with it," I insisted, hoping he believed me. "I think it's pretty. Really, I do. Please don't take any offense, but sometimes I think it just makes me sound like I'm older than I am."

"But look at you, dear," Betty exclaimed. "You're a spring chicken if I ever saw one."

"Yeah, I have to agree," Walt chimed in. "Any man I

know would take one look at you and not have a single thought that involved you being old."

I felt myself blush.

Betty swatted at Walt's shoulder and ordered, "Ignore him. If you prefer Ella or Nora, we'll call you that."

"Speak for yourself, woman. Eleanor's a classic, timeless name. A gorgeous one for a gorgeous girl."

I couldn't help but laugh at their banter. Once I managed to get myself under control, I stated, "I'm okay with whatever you want to call me. Any of the three names will work."

The memory of meeting my first real friends in town flitted out of my mind as fast as it came in. I snapped out of it and looked to Walt.

"Hi, Walt," I greeted him. "I am all stocked up, but only because it's my normal day to go shopping. It was absolute craziness out there today."

"I'm not surprised to hear that," he declared. "But it's good you're all set. I suspect you'll be grateful for that over the next few days."

Smiling at him, I agreed, "I'm sure I will. Are you and Betty good? Is there anything I can do to help either of you out?"

Walt shook his head. "We've lived here all our lives, dear. We know what to expect and prepare for the worst each time. We'll get through this one, too."

I wasn't sure if I should share that I didn't quite understand all the hysteria. Walt probably would have rallied Betty and instituted a sit-down at my place where they'd explain everything I seemed to be oblivious to. It wasn't that I'd mind a visit from them; I'd just prefer to not put them through the trouble.

"I have no doubts," I assured him. "Well, I better get inside so I can get my groceries put away. I'll talk to you later, Walt. Please tell Betty I said hello."

"Will do," he promised. "Stay warm, Eleanor."

With that, I got back in my car and drove the several hundred feet up my mostly straight but gradually inclined driveway to my home.

My home.

One that I was particularly proud to own.

This was mostly because I'd worked my butt off to be able to afford it. I didn't splurge on much, but I knew that if I was making a move, I was going to make one into a beautiful place. I drove through the neighborhood months ago and instantly fell in love. With the homes, of course. I loved mine, but there were some that were far more exquisite. Not that I'd been in any of them at the time. I just knew. Anyone who saw them would know.

What I loved most about mine was the view. That view wasn't some majestic sweeping landscape, though. It was simply a view of my favorite home in the neighborhood. The one that belonged to my next door neighbor.

My handsome, manly, sexy neighbor. I didn't know a thing about him other than the fact that he was breathtaking and that I wanted to marry him. Never in my life had I ever seen a man so rugged. And it wasn't until I saw him that I realized he was exactly the kind of man I wanted for myself.

Sure, he could have been a serial killer, but I found it unlikely.

Especially since Walt and Betty had invited me to have dinner with them and Max.

Initially, I'd agreed to dinner with them. But that was before I knew that Max would be joining us. As soon as I found out, I knew I'd have to come up with an excuse. So, on the morning of the big day, I called them to let them know I wasn't feeling well.

It wasn't exactly a lie.

The truth was, I did feel sick.

Because even though I'd seen Max from a distance, I knew he was perfect. So perfect that I was certain I'd end up making a fool of myself. I woke up that morning feeling sick to my stomach at the prospect of meeting him. Perhaps most people would have looked at that as a good thing.

I did not.

When it came to meeting new people, I didn't have a problem...especially if they made the first approach. But meeting men was something else entirely.

I'd given up long ago. I was never the type of woman who'd make the first move for fear of rejection. The thought was paralyzing. And when it came to approaching me, most men never made the move. Especially once they learned who I was.

If there were one man I'd want to make the move on me, though, it was Max. I just wasn't sure I'd ever put myself in a position for that to happen. Because if we actually did meet and he rejected me, I wasn't sure I'd be able to handle it. Anyone else, I wouldn't care. But Max was something else entirely.

So, I resolved myself to the fact that I could be happy watching him occasionally if he were outside doing work around his house. At least then I could live in a fantasy and always have hope.

After making a few trips back and forth from the garage into the house with my groceries, I unpacked them and put them away. When I finished a few minutes later, I immediately went to the television and found the news. No sooner did I sit down to listen when I heard my cell phone ringing in the other room.

I hopped up off the couch and moved back to the kitchen to retrieve it from my purse.

"Hey, Mom," I greeted after looking at the display and seeing her name there.

"Hi, Nora. I wanted to call and make sure you got your shopping done. Your father told me they're calling for a big storm up there," she replied.

I shook my head in disbelief and laughed. "Yes, I went shopping. And I'm convinced that at least half the town was at the store with me."

"I'm not surprised to hear that," she began. "They're saying it's supposed to be really bad. And if it does what they are calling for, it could be one of the worst in the state's history."

"Really?" I asked, not doing a good job hiding my surprise.

After a moment of silence, she asked, "How do you not know this, Nora?" My mother was clearly alarmed, and perhaps she was even a bit frustrated with me.

Even though she couldn't see me, I shrugged. "I don't know. I've been busy working this week."

Beyond daily email checks and minor work-related tasks, I didn't work every day. But occasionally, I'd have bigger projects that took up my time and attention. And my mother knew that when I had something like that that I was working on, I stayed focused for extended periods of time.

"Okay. Well, as long as you have everything you need to hold you over for a few days if it gets bad. Plus, even if the power goes out, you have your generator."

"Exactly," I agreed. "I'm not really worried at this point. But if it makes you feel better, I actually just turned on the television and I'm going to listen to the news reports. I'll heed all the warnings."

Hesitating a moment, my mom finally replied, "That does make me feel better. Please check in with us over the next few days. I just want to know you're okay."

I rolled my eyes at her overprotectiveness. I realized I was her daughter and only child and that I was far away, but I was still a grown adult. I often wondered if there was an age when she'd finally recognize the fact that I could take care of myself. No matter how many times I contemplated it, I always came to the same conclusion. She'd never stop worrying, so I'd always be sure to quell her fears. "I will, Mom. I'll talk to you later."

"Okay. Love you, Nora."

"Love you, too."

Disconnecting the call with my mom, I sat back down on the couch and listened to the weather reports.

Ten minutes later, I understood precisely why everyone at the store seemed to be filled with dread.

My mom was right. Apparently, this storm was expected to be serious. Because reporters were showing images of a storm that hit Maine twenty-two years ago. That storm left devastation and destruction in its wake. And the storm that was heading for us now was expected to be worse than that one.

Now, it all made sense.

The utter looks of despair and terror on the faces of everyone at the store. Walt's insistence that I'd be thankful for the provisions I'd picked up. My mom calling to check on me because even my parents knew.

I bolted up off the couch and flew into panic mode. The storm was expected to start within the next two and a half hours.

The first thing I did was run outside to check the gauge on the propane tank. Sure, I had a generator, but without any propane to run it, it wouldn't do me any good. The gauge read thirty pounds of pressure. It wasn't great, but at least it was better than nothing. I ran back inside and quickly searched online for the number to the company that would come and fill my tank. It was a few minutes past five o'clock in the evening. They had just closed. Even still, I decided to try my luck. Worst case, I'd leave a message and hopefully they'd be able to make it out to fill my tank tomorrow.

As I suspected, they didn't answer. I left a message explaining my predicament, asked them to call me back, and moved on to my next task.

As much as I had hoped I wouldn't have to do it, that task involved making a call to my parents.

"Hello?" my dad answered.

"Hey, Dad."

"Nora? What's going on, sweetheart?" he asked. "Your mom said she just talked to you."

I swallowed hard, wondering if I should even ask. I really didn't want to worry my parents, but I needed his advice.

Doing my best to keep any panic or worry out of my tone, I replied, "Yeah. I just had a question for you, though. I was watching the weather reports and realized that they're anticipating extended power outages with this storm that's heading this way. I hadn't realized they were expecting it to be so severe. Anyway, it got me thinking about my generator and the propane I have in the tank. I just went out to check the gauge, and I've only got thirty pounds of pressure. How long do you think that'll last me?"

"That was a standard size tank, from what I recall. Thirty pounds of pressure remaining in a hundred-gallon tank…" He trailed off. "Nora, I can't say for sure, but probably anywhere from eight to twelve hours depending on the electric draw and your specific generator."

Oh no.

Based on reports, people were without power for at least a week twenty years ago. Some went longer than that. Especially those who were farther away from town.

People like me.

"Right," I answered cheerfully, not wanting to alarm him. "Good to know."

"You're scared, Nori," he immediately responded, evidently picking up on my nervousness.

Damn.

He always knew. No matter how hard I tried to hide it, my dad always knew when I was worried. And I knew he knew when he called me Nori.

"Dad," I whispered.

"Darling, listen," he began. "You're Eleanor Page. You're my daughter, and you are going to be fine. Call the gas company and get on their schedule for the first available spot they have open. If your power goes out, conserve your resources. Don't use your electricity unless it's absolutely necessary. Heat is a necessity; watching movies is not. Your mom told me you went to the store and stocked up on food. If you can make extra meals tonight, do it. The stove will have a larger electric draw than the microwave. If you can avoid using both by getting by on things that you won't need to heat up, that's even better. And since everything in that house is electric, Nora, you should probably fill at least one of your bathtubs with water. You'll be able to flush your toilets that way."

"Right," I stated, making mental notes of everything he was telling me. "Got it."

"Good. Now, go take care of everything I just told you and relax. No matter what happens, you'll be fine. You've done things much harder than this."

I couldn't help but smile. I loved my dad's confidence in my abilities, even if I sometimes believed he was embellishing them.

"Love you, Dad."

"You too, Nora. Keep us in the loop."

"I will."

We disconnected, and I got to work.

I plugged in all of my electronics, including my phone and my laptop, to make sure everything that ran on battery power was fully charged. Then, I went about making dinner and preparing a few extra meals. After, I filled up a bathtub in one of the guest bathrooms.

Once I completed all of the things on my dad's checklist, I hopped in the shower and got ready for bed. I crawled under my blankets and popped on a movie. Through it, I heard the freezing rain as it hit the windows. The wind howled for what seemed like hours.

And it was three hours after the storm began when my power went out. My generator turned on, but I turned off everything. The only thing running was my heating system.

As I listened to the storm raging outside my window, I knew.

This wasn't going to be just any ordinary storm.

This was going to be a storm that changed lives.

CHAPTER 2

Max

THE ROARING SOUND OF GENERATORS RUNNING IN THE neighborhood was suddenly drowned out by a rumbling engine coming up my driveway.

I looked up from the large tree branch that had fallen just shy of the corner of my garage to the opposite end of the driveway. That's when I saw my neighbor from across the street heading my way. Leave it to Walt to be out on a four-wheeler in weather conditions like this.

The freezing rain and ice had fallen all night. Other than what I saw from out my windows and by standing outside, I didn't know the extent of the damage across town. Even still, I had a feeling it was substantial.

We were currently experiencing the brief and necessary respite from the storm, but it wasn't expected to last long.

"Everything okay?" I asked when he cut off the engine.

"Yeah, but you know me. I don't like sitting still, so I've got to get out and check out the damage. At least until the snow starts up and we're locked inside again."

I laughed. If that wasn't the truth. Walt might have been in his late sixties, but that didn't stop him. He got around and did things as though he were still in his twenties.

"Good thing you've got studded tires and chains on your four-wheeler, Walt," I joked.

He shrugged it off.

"Do you need any help with that one?" Walt asked, pointing to the tree branch as he walked over in my direction.

"If you don't mind," I replied. As Walt moved closer to the opposite end of the branch, I added, "It didn't seem to matter that the closest trees aren't close enough to land here. That wind was brutal last night."

Walt bent down to grab his end while I wrapped my hands around mine. "Tell me about it," he agreed. "I was just hoping we weren't going to end up with a tree through one of our windows."

Once we moved the branch far enough from the house off to the opposite side of the driveway, I asked, "How did you and Betty fare last night?"

"We're good. The generator kicked on last night, and we've been solid ever since. Betty's been glued to the television watching the news."

"I haven't checked it yet," I admitted. "I'm guessing it's bad everywhere."

"Worse," he confirmed. "And because they don't know what's going to happen now that the snow hasn't hit yet, they're expecting we're going to be waiting even longer for the power to be restored. Forget about getting out to clear the roads. They said there are so many trees down all over that the plows and salt trucks would never be able to get through."

I shook my head. "It's like we're reliving that storm from twenty-two years ago."

I might have been fifteen when that storm hit, but I remember it like it happened yesterday. It resulted in so much destruction, we were rebuilding for months afterward.

"It seems that way," Walt said. "In fact, it's looking like it might surpass it in terms of damage. Obviously, we won't know until the snow comes and goes."

"Well, you know I'm here if you and Betty need anything," I offered.

Walt let out a laugh. "It's not us that I'm worried about."

My brows pulled together in confusion.

Realizing I had no clue what he meant by that statement, he threw his thumb over his shoulder and clarified, "It's the one over there that concerns me."

He was pointing in the direction of my neighbor's house. Given the amount of land each of our houses sat on, that home was easily still a good thousand feet away from mine. And it didn't sit back off the main road as far as mine did.

"What do you mean?" I asked.

Walt chuckled and retorted, "How is it possible that you know just about every single person in this town, but you haven't yet met your next-door neighbor?"

I honestly had no idea. Walt and Betty had spoken

about her several times, but I hadn't yet had the opportunity to meet her. Of course, I knew I should have gone over and introduced myself and welcomed her to the neighborhood when she arrived, but my company was in the middle of a huge project at the time. I was gone early in the mornings and didn't return until late in the evening. By the time I finished that project, she'd already been here for more than a month. Foolishly, I had expected I'd see her out at some point, but I never did.

"I don't know, Walt," I answered truthfully. "But that's beside the point. Why are you so worried about her?"

"It's not just me," he began. "Betty is, too. Eleanor's a young girl, and she's from Florida. Not only is she not used to the harsh winters like this, she also doesn't have any family here to look out for her."

My head dropped to one side as my eyes moved from Walt's face to my elusive neighbor's house. Eleanor. I'd just learned more about her in a five-minute conversation with Walt than I had in the last three months since she moved here.

It was then I decided that making the effort to go over and introduce myself would be the right thing to do, even if it was going to happen a lot later than it should have.

I was just about to tell Walt that I'd run over and check on Eleanor before the storm picked back up again, but before I had the opportunity to say anything, my attention was pulled to the sound of another vehicle coming up my driveway. My eyes left Eleanor's house and went to the black pickup truck that was now just a few feet away.

Our neighbor, Cody, who lived a few doors down from me on Walt's side of the road stepped out.

"Hey, Max. Walt," he greeted us.

"Cody, hey. What's going on?"

A frustrated look came over him. "Molly and I had a tree fall on the detached garage last night. I was hoping you might be able to lend a hand. Molly's all fired up to help me with it before the snow hits, but well, we just found out she's pregnant. I don't want her getting hurt."

"Congratulations, man. That's great news. Sorry about the garage, though," I said.

"Thanks," he replied.

"Yeah, I can come help. Do I need to bring any equipment?" I asked.

Cody shook his head. "No, Bob is there now with Tom. We just need a bit more manpower."

"I'll follow you," Walt declared.

"I'm coming right behind the both of you," I added.

"Thanks, guys." With that, Cody turned around and got back in his truck. Walt followed him back down the driveway.

I turned and ran back into my house, added another layer of clothing and some work gloves before I got in my truck and took off down the road.

Just over two hours later, with five of us working in the bitter cold temps, we'd managed to remove the large tree and board up the garage. It wasn't a permanent fix, but I made sure it was at least sturdy enough to hopefully withstand the remainder of the storm.

Once I'd pulled back into the garage at my house, I got out of the truck and started to round the back of the vehicle. I hadn't yet closed the garage door, so when I moved past the tailgate, I heard something that just didn't sound right.

Stopping and redirecting myself, I stepped out into the driveway and listened closer.

It took me only a few seconds to figure out what the noise was. There was a generator running but just barely. And it was coming from the direction of Eleanor's house. From what I could tell at the distance, it sounded like the generator was almost out of gas. If it had been anyone else, I'd have thought there was another problem because we all knew to have our tanks topped off. If what Walt said was true, and Eleanor was from Florida, it was likely she had no idea how severe a storm in northern Maine could be.

Knowing that it was easily going to be several days before the power was back or the roads could be traveled, I did what I had to do. I didn't even get in my truck. I walked the distance down my driveway, through the trees and grass between our homes, and right up to her front door. It wasn't an easy trek considering the amount of ice that we got, but I managed to get there without an injury. While I was on my way to Eleanor's house, the generator had officially given up.

I rang the doorbell and waited.

When the door opened, I was nearly knocked on my ass. I never expected what I saw.

Staring back at me was the most beautiful woman I'd ever laid my eyes on. Her piercing green eyes widened in shock as she stared silently at me. I took a moment to note her delicate features—a slender nose, perfectly-shaped pink lips, and exquisite eyes. She had blonde hair that landed right at the top swells of her full breasts. Sadly, I couldn't see the rest of her body because she was wrapped up in a huge, fuzzy blanket.

My eyes were diverted right back to her gorgeous lips when she spoke. "Hi. Can I help you?" she asked.

I quickly blinked away my surprise that I had this treasure of a woman living right next to me all this time that I'd never seen before. I wanted to kick my own ass for not coming over to meet her sooner.

"Yeah, hi. My name is Max, and I'm your neighbor," I introduced myself.

She didn't respond. In fact, it looked like she was struggling with something because I noticed her take a deep swallow.

"You're Eleanor, right?" I asked.

Her lips parted the moment I said her name. I didn't want her thinking I was some creepy stalker, so I added, "Walt mentioned your name to me earlier this morning."

She stood there staring at me but still said nothing. Sensing her uneasiness, I went on, "I was just down the road with Walt and a few of the other neighbors helping with the removal of a tree that fell on one of their garages. When I came back, I heard your generator. It sounds like it just ran out of gas."

Finally, she spoke. "Um, yeah. It just happened. I

didn't realize until it was too late yesterday that it was so low. When I checked the gauge yesterday, I only had thirty pounds of pressure left."

That confirmed my suspicions that she hadn't known what to expect with a storm here. "Right, well, I wanted to let you know that I've got plenty of room at my place if you need somewhere warm to stay for a few nights until your tank can be refilled."

She shifted uncomfortably and insisted, "Oh, that's really kind of you, but I don't want to intrude." She lifted her hand up and waved her cell phone at me. "Besides, I was just going to call the gas company again to see if they'd be able to make an emergency visit for me today."

I shook my head, not excited about the fact that I was going to have to break the news to her. "I hate to tell you this, but nobody is getting on the roads today, darling. There are trees down everywhere from the ice and the wind gusts. And considering the blizzard-like conditions are going to be heading this way in the next hour or so, I'm willing to bet they won't be coming out today."

"Oh. Well, I'll try them anyway. If I don't have any luck, I'm sure the power will be back on soon. I appreciate the offer, though. Thank you."

"Eleanor? Can I call you that?" I asked.

She nodded and added, "Or Ella or Nora."

I smiled and said softly, "Ella."

Ella didn't answer.

I took one step closer to her, my voice dropped, and I explained, "The temps are going to drop below zero tonight. With the number of windows you've got in this place, if you don't have your heat on, it's going to get unbearably cold really quick."

Ella stood up straighter and maintained, "I'm sure I'll be alright as long as I can keep the heat that I do have in here."

She wanted me out of her doorway.

Deciding I wouldn't make a good first impression if I forced her out of her home, I acquiesced, "Okay. But just in case you change your mind, let me give you my number. It'll make me feel better to know that you can at least get in touch with me if you need something. The offer stands if you need me. I suspect we'll all be home for the next few days."

She seemed to be receptive to that idea, so I gave her my number and watched as she programmed it into her phone.

At that, she thanked me once again.

"After I leave, make sure you write that number down somewhere," I instructed.

She looked confused by that statement, but said, "Okay."

By the time night fell and a good ten inches of snow had already fallen, I tried my best but failed. I couldn't stop myself from worrying about her.

So when I climbed in bed that night, I had a hard time finding sleep. All I could think about was Ella being cold and alone in her house. It wasn't until I promised myself that I'd get up and check on her first thing in the morning that I was finally able to drift.

Eleanor

I needed a miracle.

Or divine intervention.

As cold as it was outside, I was burning up. Part of the reason for this was because I was currently pacing in my great room. Mostly, though, it was because Max had just been here.

At my house.

Standing at my front door.

I didn't know how to process this. I couldn't even begin to manage what I was feeling about having him mere feet away from me. I could have even reached out and touched him. I should have. I know I certainly wanted to.

But he was...wow, he was incredible. Big. So big. I felt like a small child standing next to him. He was tall and built and so very handsome.

And he came to offer me a place to stay for a few days, I thought. I could barely control my excitement.

The minute I closed the door, I ran through my house and over to the window in my office. It looked out across the property toward Max's house. That's when I realized he had walked over here. He trudged through the slick ice and unforgiving cold just to offer me a warm bed to sleep in for a few days.

As much as I wanted to take him up on it, I simply couldn't. I could barely get two words out when he was standing on my doorstep. There was no way I'd be able to handle essentially living with him until the storm passed and power was restored.

But boy did I wish I could have. Because Max was dreamy. So much so that if I hadn't already decided on it months ago when I moved here, I would have decided now. I was going to marry Max.

Of course, that was purely a dream. I didn't actually believe that would happen for a multitude of reasons. The biggest of those was not the usual reason, which was the truth of who I was. This time it was merely the fact that the sight of him had rendered me speechless. I didn't think a successful marriage could be built without communication.

In an effort to calm myself down, I decided to stop looking out the window at him as he walked back to his place. Instead, I chose to follow through on what I told Max I was going to do. I tried contacting the gas company. There was, once again, no answer. It hit me then that I was going to be in a very dire situation if I couldn't get this figured out.

There was simply no way, no way at all, that I could go to Max's house.

So, I needed a distraction.

Since I had no electricity, I had to find a way to occupy myself.

Food.

Food would do the trick. I dashed out to the kitchen and made a sandwich. I took my time eating it, but sadly, the food didn't help.

Work.

I went back to my office, pulled out my laptop, which was still fully charged, and worked for a bit. Once I'd finished that task, which had distracted me for quite a while, I moved on to something else.

Entertainment.

Since anything involving electronics was out of the question, I snatched a book off my bookshelf and curled up in the corner of my sitting room. Every so often, I'd pull up my phone and check my emails or social media news feeds. It kept me so distracted I hadn't paid attention to the battery life. By the time I noticed, I'd drained a substantial amount of it.

The hours had passed, more snow than I'd ever seen in my life had fallen, and the power never came back on. After I ate dinner that evening, which consisted of a turkey and cheese sandwich with a side of chips, all of the warm and fuzzy feelings I felt about Max earlier in the day were gone, sadly.

Because just as he said would happen, the temperature dropped drastically. And it was freezing. I pulled on more layers, grabbed a bunch of extra blankets, and lit a dozen or so candles. Hours later, approaching bedtime, I found myself wishing I hadn't been such a fool. I knew then that I should've taken Max up on his offer.

Without any other options, I put on a pair of boots, grabbed my keys, and walked out the door.

I made it a few steps before I admitted to myself that I'd never make it to Max's house. The snow had to have been at least a foot deep and was lying on top of a sheet of ice. With each step I took, I slipped. Once, I even went down in the snow. Visibility was reduced to almost nothing, and the snow was whipping fast around me. That was my cue to turn around and go back into my house.

Unable to stand it any longer, I grabbed my phone and pulled up Max's name. But before I could touch my finger to it, the screen went blank, and the phone died.

I lit my candles again, hoping they'd produce some heat. Using the light from them, I slipped out of my wet clothing and put on a fresh pair of leggings and warm sweats. Then, I bundled myself up as tight as I could in the tangle of blankets.

It took some time, but I eventually stopped shivering.

CHAPTER 3

Max

I WAS GENERALLY AN EARLY RISER, BUT USUALLY ONLY EVER woke up this early because I had to get up and go to work. Never have I ever woken up because I was feeling particularly troubled about the well-being of my neighbor. Sure, I felt some level of responsibility to the residents of my community, but none had ever affected me like Eleanor.

No sooner did I open my eyes when I realized I still heard the distant hum of my generator. I hadn't expected the power would have come back on, but I was hoping by some miracle it would. And that was all because I knew Ella was right next door, and she was in the cold.

I bolted up in bed and looked outside. So much snow had fallen and it still hadn't stopped. I didn't have to look at the thermostat to know that the temperature outside was well below freezing...probably even sub-zero.

Knowing that Ella's generator had run out of gas

just before I went over there yesterday, I knew I had to follow through on the promise I made to myself last night. I had to go back over and check on her. I quickly got dressed, layered up, added a hat, coat, and gloves, and walked outside. Almost instantly, I felt the blistering sting of the cold air on the exposed skin on my face. The snow came up to my knees in spots that hadn't drifted. The depth of the snow made movement difficult, but I trudged through just to get to her.

It took some time, much longer than I would have liked, but I eventually found myself ringing Eleanor's doorbell. As I waited for her to come to the door and open it, I turned around and looked out at my neighborhood. It was devoid of any color. Fresh, white snow covered every surface. I had no doubts that clean up would last for quite some time after the storm ended.

When too much time had gone by without an answer, I pounded my fist against Eleanor's door several times.

More time than I was comfortable with passed when I finally heard the deadbolt on the door. A second later, the door opened.

"Jesus, Ella," I breathed, my throat tight. One look at her and I knew she hadn't managed the night very well. She looked exhausted. I pulled my hand out of my glove and touched the skin on her cheek. She felt like ice. "Why didn't you call me?" I asked.

Instinctively, her neck craned and she pushed her cheek harder into my hand. "I tried," she started, her voice just a hair over a whisper. "But my phone died."

Without an invitation and knowing this wasn't the time for a debate, I stepped inside her house, closed the door, and ordered, "You're not staying here."

"Okay," she immediately agreed.

"We've got to get you warmed up, so let's get a bag packed quickly. I've got everything you'll need other than clothes."

She stared up at me, silent and unmoving.

"Ella?" I called.

"Hmm?" she responded.

"A bag, darling," I prompted. When she still made no move to do anything, I stepped closer and clipped, "Fuck it, I've got clothes. Are the keys to your house in your car?"

She shook her head and said, "On the island."

I moved past her in the direction of her kitchen, snatched up her keys, and came back to find her still standing in the same spot.

Pulling my hat off my head, I slipped it onto hers and made sure her ears were covered. She was wrapped in a blanket, so her hands were protected, and I saw she had a pair of thick wool socks on her feet. I bent slightly to put one of my arms behind her knees and the other behind her back before I lifted her. As adamant as she'd been yesterday when I arrived to offer her a place to stay, she didn't put up a fight at all today.

After I managed to lock her front door, I trekked through the deep snow back to my house. The minute we were inside and I set Ella back down on her feet, she began trembling.

"Do you like tea, Ella?"

She tilted her head back to look up at me and whispered her reply. "Yeah."

Before I had the chance to turn the tea kettle on, Ella took a step toward me. Her arms were bent at the elbows, her hands balled into tight, little fists clutching the blanket at the front of her chest. She pressed her cheek against my chest and shivered. I did the only thing I could do and ran my hands up and down her arms and back.

A few minutes had passed when she rasped, "It's so cold."

"I know. We're going to get you warmed up," I assured her.

Her body shook harder. So, I picked her up again, carried her out of the kitchen into my family room. After setting her down on the couch, I covered her with a heavy, wool blanket. Then, I moved to the fireplace, turned it on, and removed my boots. As quickly as I could, I ran upstairs, pulled on a pair of dry sweatpants, and made my way back to her.

Ella's teeth were chattering hard and fast while her body trembled uncontrollably; she was still so cold. I lifted the edge of the blanket and was about to slip underneath it when she asked, "What...are you doing?"

Settling myself on the couch, my body running the length of hers, I answered, "Body heat."

Instead of protesting, she immediately shifted her body closer to mine. I held her as she shuddered for a long time until the quakes became less violent, her teeth stopped chattering, and her limbs began loosening up.

Eventually, she pulled her face, which had been buried in my chest, away and tilted her head back to look up at me. Keeping her wrapped in my arms, I smiled at her. Ella's eyes dropped to my mouth for a split second before she murmured, "Thank you."

"My pleasure," I asserted. When she said nothing else, I declared, "It's breakfast time. Does French toast work for you?"

"Yeah."

With that, Ella and I got up off the couch and moved out to the kitchen. While I worked to get the food made, she asked, "Can I do something to help?"

"The coffee is on a timer, so that's good to go. You can grab mugs in the cabinet above the pot. I'll take cream and one sugar. And if you want to turn on the tea kettle, knock yourself out. Otherwise, have a seat."

"If it's okay with you, I think I'd prefer the coffee this morning," she shared. "I didn't sleep much last night."

Guilty was the only word to describe how I felt. She spent the night freezing, shivering, and awake, while I slept in my bed, warm and comfortable.

I turned toward her and insisted, "Help yourself, darling. There's more than enough."

Ella made quick work of pouring and serving coffee. Once she was seated at the island, I noted, "So it seems like you decided not to listen and write my number down."

"I did," she argued.

"So why didn't you call?"

She looked at me in disbelief. "I told you my cell phone died. With my generator not running, I had no power to charge it. How would I have called you?"

"Landline?"

Shaking her head like I was speaking a foreign language, she challenged, "You're joking, right? Who has a landline these days?"

I twisted my neck and looked in the direction of the phone sitting on the end of my countertop.

Ella's eyes narrowed and she blurted, "Exactly how old are you?"

My head jerked back in surprise. Given how reserved she'd been since I first met her, I hadn't expected that from her.

She looked mortified.

"Oh my God. I'm so sorry," she lamented. "That was rude of me."

I couldn't stop myself from doubling over with laughter. Once I managed to pull myself together, I flipped the toast on the griddle and teased, "I didn't realize having a way to communicate with the outside world made me old."

"It doesn't," she tried to convince me. "It's just that there aren't a lot of people who still have landlines these days. I mean, I've convinced my mom that she doesn't need one anymore, but my father's holding on to it for reasons I can't comprehend."

My brows shot up, silently questioning her. "Uh, I'm just going to point out that had you had a landline, you could have called me. Though, I guess if you had come

32

here with me the first time I came over there, you could have avoided this whole mess."

She sighed and shook her head in disappointment. "That was so foolish of me," she admitted. "It didn't take long for me to realize how big of a mistake I made. By the time I made the decision to take you up on your offer, it was just before ten o'clock last night. I walked outside and only took a few steps before I realized I'd never make it over here. It was too icy, too dark, and I couldn't see anything. After I slipped and fell a few times, I knew I was taking a big risk. I didn't want to freeze to death in the snow. So, I went back inside my house and pulled up your number to call you, but just as I was about to touch your name on the screen, the phone died."

Fuck.

She needed me last night. She had reached her breaking point hours before I came back to check on her.

Guilt speared through me again.

I stood there, staring at her beautiful face, feeling grateful I didn't walk into something worse than I did this morning.

"Max?" she called.

The sound of her voice calling my name snapped me out of my thoughts. My eyes went to hers and I noted the tension in her body. Once there, she asked, "Is everything okay?"

"Hours," I stated.

"What?"

Shaking my head at the disgust I felt in myself, I explained, "You needed me for hours, and I had no idea. Do you know how many times I talked myself out of walking back over to your place last night so I could drag you back here where you'd be warm?"

Her shoulders fell as she relaxed again. "I'm good now, though. Besides, like you said, I could have accepted your help the first time you showed up on my doorstep."

My gaze dropped to the French toast. I slipped the spatula under the last two pieces and put them on a plate. Truthfully, I needed the distraction. Because if I allowed myself to think about it, I'd become even more consumed with regret and guilt than I already was.

I slid a plate, syrup, and powdered sugar in front of Ella. "Eat, darling," I ordered.

Once I was seated next to her and we'd both taken a couple of bites of our breakfast, she said, "I have a bit of a problem."

"What's wrong?" I wondered.

"Well, it's just that you carried me over here, so I have no shoes," she explained.

"You don't need shoes right now if you're just going to be in my house," I pointed out.

"I know that, but I need to go back to my house," she argued.

I gave her a look that I hoped conveyed the message that she absolutely would not be going back to her house until the power was back on or, at the very least, her generator was up and running again. Ella didn't seem the least bit fazed by my look, so I warned, "You're not going back to your house."

"Excuse me?" she challenged, turning her body on the stool toward mine.

"Ella, I'm not trying to hold you hostage here, but you can't stay there until the storm passes and you at least have working heat again."

When she didn't respond, I turned my head in her direction and found her looking at me. "What?" I asked.

She nervously bit her lip. "Nothing. I think you misunderstood me, though. I'm not looking to go back home to stay there right now, but I need to get my phone and charger so I can call my parents."

"I've got a phone you can use," I offered.

"Okay, but I don't have any clothes here either," she noted.

I couldn't help but laugh again. "I'm not sure if you remember this, but I tried to get you to pack a bag before I brought you here. You were a zombie. Actually, that's wrong. Zombies move. You were like a statue."

Ella dropped her gaze to her lap briefly. "I was so cold," she whispered when she looked back at me again.

My fork clattered to the plate, and I reached out to curl my hand along the side of her neck. My thumb stroked along her jaw as I returned just as softly, "I know, baby."

I noticed Ella's breathing had changed. Short, quick, nervous breaths were all she seemed to be able to manage at that moment. Sensing what was happening, I pulled my hand away and conceded, "There's supposed to be another break in the storm around lunchtime. If you want to give me a list, I can run over and grab your things."

"Um, well, I'm not exactly sure we're at the stage in our relationship where I should be letting you root through my undergarments. I mean, I just met you yesterday," she reasoned.

I cocked an eyebrow. "But you are saying we might get to that stage at some point?" I teased.

Shock registered all over Ella's face. "I did *not* say that!" she shrieked.

I loved seeing her like this. She might not have wanted to admit it, but I was clearly seeing the attraction between us wasn't just one-sided. She felt something, too.

"Right," I said, my tone indicating I didn't believe her. "Fine. If you want to call your parents sooner, you can use my phone. We'll keep our eye on the snow and when it slows down a bit, I'll carry you back to your place so you can grab your things."

"Thank you," she said.

Standing from my seat, I reached over and grabbed her empty plate. "Don't mention it," I insisted.

Ella and I worked together to clean up the breakfast dishes. As soon as we finished, I got my phone and held it out to her. "If you want to call your parents now, you can use my phone," I offered.

She took the phone and tapped on the screen. I started to walk out of the room to give her some privacy. But it wasn't before I heard her say, "It's me, Mom. I'm okay."

Ten minutes later, Ella came in and sat down on the opposite end of the couch where I was sitting watching the news. She set the phone down on the coffee table and said, "Thanks for letting me borrow your phone. I just turned thirty-one, but my parents worry about me like I'm still ten."

I grinned at her.

"What's that look for?"

"You *just* turned thirty-one," I repeated her statement.

"Yeah."

Still grinning, I slowly shook my head and stated, "You're just a baby."

She cocked an eyebrow. "Thirty-one hardly makes me a baby. Though, I guess it really all depends on you, old man."

"I'll be thirty-seven this year," I told her.

"Really?" she asked, her shock clear as day.

My eyes narrowed. "I'm not sure how to take your obvious astonishment right now."

She shrugged. "You don't look anywhere close to thirty-seven. You act your age, maybe even older, especially considering the landline, but you definitely don't look it."

Chuckling, I approved, "I'll take that as a compliment."

After a moment of silence, I asked, "Your parents were worried?"

Nodding, she explained, "Yeah. They live in Florida, so they're not unaccustomed to bad storms. It's just that they're used to the ones of the high wind and rain variety, not the ice and snow kind. That combined with the fact that I'm so far away they can't get to me in a situation like this makes it hard for them."

"Did you grow up in Florida?" I questioned her.

"Yeah, I lived there all my life," she shared.

I lived here all my life, so I couldn't imagine why she'd ever leave. Before I had a chance to ask her why she left, she went on, "But I wasn't happy there. I love my parents and my friends, so it was difficult to leave them behind. What about you? Have you always lived here?"

The more she spoke, the more intriguing I found Ella to be. And I was discovering that the more she shared, the more I wanted to know. "Born and raised," I replied with a nod of my head. "If you don't mind me asking, why did you leave Florida? If we're talking about climate, you couldn't have chosen a place to move to that was any less similar to what you were used to."

Ella took in a deep breath and sighed, "I wanted some solace. We lived in West Palm Beach. Miami wasn't far away, and it's a huge tourist destination. I have my friends, but I honestly didn't like the crowds."

"And you were able to relocate here without an issue for work?" I asked.

She let out a small laugh and answered, "Pretty much, considering I'm my own boss."

"No kidding?" I marveled. "A fellow entrepreneur then? What do you do?"

"I am an app developer."

I blinked my eyes in surprise. "I'm sorry?"

"Mobile apps," she semi-repeated. "You know, like you'd find on smart devices, like phones and tablets."

I reached over to the coffee table and swiped my phone from the top of it. Holding it out to her, I wondered, "Do I have any of your apps on my phone?"

Ella's entire demeanor changed. She suddenly seemed very nervous as her eyes shifted to anything other than me. The next thing I knew, she shot up from her seat on the couch and gasped, "Look! The snow has stopped. We should probably head over to my place to grab my things before it starts falling again."

Sure enough, I looked outside and saw that we were, in fact, experiencing a lull in the snowfall.

"Looks like it," I affirmed as I stood and moved toward her. "Before we head over there, do you know what you need? It's still very cold out there, and I just got you warmed up. I'm more than happy to do it again, but I'm thinking it's not great that we keep putting your body through that kind of trauma."

A sultry look came over her, giving me all the affirmation I needed that she was into me. As quickly as it was there, it was gone. "How many days do you think it's going to be before either the power is back on or the gas company is going to get out here to refill my propane tank?" she asked.

I took in a deep breath as I considered the answer to her question. "My best guess is that your tank will be filled before the power is back, but I think it could be a solid three or four days at best before they can get out here."

Her eyes widened in shock. "Wow. Are you sure it's okay that I stay here for that long?"

I shook my head and replied, "No, actually. I'm going to need you out in two days. Do you think you'll be able to find other accommodations?"

Her lips parted, and she stared at me for a moment before she mumbled, "Um, yeah...I'll just see if I can get to a hotel. Hopefully the roads will be cleared by then."

I moved closer to her, threw my arm around her shoulder, and pulled her close. "Ella, darling, I was just joking with you. You're welcome to stay as long as you'd like."

She tipped her head back and looked up at me. Her voice was just barely a whisper when she said, "That wasn't very nice."

"So you can call me an old man, but I can't tease you?" I challenged her. "That doesn't seem fair."

The tension left Ella's body as she rolled her eyes at me. Brushing it off, she asked, "Do you have a piece of paper and a pen so I can make a list of what I need to get?"

I gave her a quick squeeze before I responded, "You've got it."

Then, I went in search of paper and a pen.

CHAPTER 4

Eleanor

"THAT SHOULD DO IT," MAX ASSERTED AS HE PULLED the warm and fuzzy winter hat down over my ears.

"I think you're overdoing it," I advised. "We're only going a couple hundred feet away. I realize it's going to be in the snow and the cold, but it's not like we'll be outside that long."

"Maybe not," he agreed. "But based on the length of that list you made, I'm guessing we're going to be in your house for a little bit while you pack all of that up. And it's not going to be much warmer in there than it's going to be outside."

I huffed. "Fine. Can we go now?" I asked him.

Max looked me over from head-to-toe and decided he'd done a sufficient job in bundling me up. "I guess it'll do."

When he carried me over earlier this morning, I only had on my layers of clothes, thick wool socks, and a blanket. Now, I had on those same clothes and socks with the addition of one of Max's hats, a scarf, an entirely-too-big jacket, and a pair of gloves. He also doubled up my socks.

I found him to be incredibly sweet and charming. The concern and care he showed me from the moment he showed up at my door this morning was something I'd miss about being home in Florida. Something I'd always gotten from my parents. But what made it better with Max was the way he climbed under the blanket and used his body to warm mine. It was, by and large, the best experience I'd had since arriving in White Pine.

As much as I used to sit in my office and look at him whenever he was outside working on his house or his landscaping, there was something incredible about being near him and talking to him. There was no denying he was amazing from a distance. But up close and personal was even better. Way, way better.

Max reached out to curl his long fingers around my arm and tugged me in his direction. He ushered us through the house and out into the garage. After getting the garage door opener out of one of his trucks, Max opened the garage door. He stood at the edge of the garage behind the truck and ordered, "Hop on."

I wasn't sure I heard him correctly. "Pardon?" I responded.

"Hop on," he repeated.

I dropped my head to one side and asked, "What do you mean?"

"I'm going to carry you over to your place," Max remarked, giving me information I already knew. "To do that, you've got to hop up and get on my back."

It took everything in me not to burst out laughing. I succeeded in holding it back and asked, "Are you telling me you're going to give me a piggyback ride?"

"Would you prefer to wrap your legs around me from the front so we're chest to chest?" he retorted, as he gave me a devilish grin. "Because that works for me, too."

My eyes nearly fell out of my head. I enjoyed Max's teasing, but I didn't know how to react when someone like him made it very clear that he was attracted to me. At least, I hoped that's what he meant to imply.

As much as I would have loved to be wrapped around him like that, I wasn't sure it was a good idea.

So, to save face, I simply claimed, "I was just concerned about your back. You know, at your age I hear that's one of the first things to go."

"You better watch it," he warned playfully taking a step toward me. His voice dipped low when he promised, "You keep it up and I'll have no problem showing you how fully functional my *entire* old-man body is."

I swallowed hard, obviously unprepared for his comeback.

After a beat of silence, he pressed, "What? No response to that?"

I narrowed my eyes at him and ordered, "Turn around, old man."

A smug look washed over Max's face. He won that argument and had no problem gloating, either. He turned around and crouched down a bit so I could get a better grip on his shoulders. Once I hopped up, Max

43

stepped out into the deep snow and pressed the button on his garage door opener to close the door before he slipped it into his pocket.

Then, with his arms holding me up under my legs, my chest pressed to his back, Max trudged through the snow. It wasn't easy considering how deep it was, and it took a lot longer than I had initially expected. When we'd made it about halfway to my place, I began to fret. "I'm sorry. Maybe we should turn around. I didn't realize just how deep the snow was. You've got to be so tired."

"Ella?" he called.

"Yeah?" I answered.

"I've got far more stamina than you're giving me credit for right now," he assured me. "If you need me to prove that to you when we're back at my place, I'm more than willing."

I snapped my mouth shut.

When I didn't respond, he muttered, "I see that works."

"What?" I asked.

"Nothing," he replied. "We're almost there. I'm taking my time because I'm trying to keep you out of the snow."

"Okay."

I figured since he was doing all the work and not complaining about it, I'd keep quiet and let him focus. And in doing that, I noticed that what he said had been exactly the case. Despite the amount of snow, Max could have easily gone a bit faster. I had no doubts that he would have if I wasn't on his back. He was taking his time because some of the snow had drifted, and it was deeper in a few spots. Whenever he reached a spot where the snow was a bit higher, I watched him hoist my legs a little higher so my feet wouldn't end up in it. I found it to be incredibly thoughtful of him.

A few minutes later, we were at my front door. Once we were inside, I realized what Max said was true. There wasn't much of a difference between the temperature in my house and outside in the snow.

"Alright," he began as he gently set me down on my feet. "Before you take off to get your things, can you show me where the door to your basement is?"

I found it to be an odd request, so I questioned him. "Why?"

"How about we save the questions for when we're on our way back to my house?" he suggested. "I'll explain then."

"Right," I agreed on a nod.

I led Max through my house to the basement door. Then, I took off upstairs to my bedroom. I packed as quickly as I could. Fifteen minutes later, I'd managed to get my clothes, sneakers, and a few toiletries I didn't suspect Max would have into a bag. I also packed my laptop and cell phone, along with their chargers, and a game. I didn't know if Max was the type or if he'd even be interested in playing, but I figured it couldn't hurt to have something for entertainment just in case.

When I made it back downstairs, I dropped my bag at the front door and found Max in my kitchen.

"Looks like you stocked up right before the storm

hit. It's cold enough in the house that I don't think you'll need to worry about anything really spoiling, but if there's something you want to bring with you, feel free. Otherwise, I've got plenty to cover the both of us."

I suddenly had an idea. I ran over and grabbed one of my environmentally-friendly reusable grocery bags and started loading up with the items I knew I'd need. Max didn't seem to be the least bit bothered by the fact that I was taking longer to gather up a few extra things that I hadn't originally planned on bringing.

Once I'd gotten everything packed up, I slipped on my snow boots. Max and I made our way to the front door where he turned and confirmed, "Got everything?"

"I think so."

With that, he took both bags from me and walked out. After I locked up, Max and I trekked back through the snow toward his place. Even though I didn't have the pleasure of hitching a ride on his back on our journey from my house to his, the return trip was just as sweet. This was because Max had my bag filled with clothes, toiletries, and electronics slung over his left shoulder, the grocery bag in his left hand, and my hand in his right.

That's right.

Max held my hand as we walked back to his house. It was the sweetest gesture, and it made me feel so special. In fact, nearly everything he'd done from the moment I met him was sweet. Even in the moments he was teasing me, I found him to be exceedingly charismatic.

"So, the good news is you won't need to worry

about any of your pipes bursting," Max stated as we cut through the trees that separated my property from his.

"What?"

"At your house," he began. "When I went down in the basement, I was checking out the water lines. The house was built back when they were making a change in a lot of homes from the standard copper pipes for plumbing to polyethylene tubing. It's far more durable than copper piping and is a lot more forgiving if the lines freeze. I turned on a few of your faucets so they'll drip water slowly. That'll help relieve the pressure in the pipes if ice does form."

Well, that was nice of him to do. I wouldn't have even thought about that, mostly because I didn't even know it was a thing that should be done.

"Does that happen?" I wondered.

"It can," he confirmed. "And it's a disaster if it does."

I did not need to be dealing with a disaster after all of this. Feeling appreciative of his mindfulness, I stated, "Thank you for doing that for me."

Apparently, living in northern Maine all his life meant that Max had learned a thing or two about how to survive the harsh winters. I was grateful he was sharing his wisdom with me.

We finally made it back to his place, but despite the snow boots that I'd been wearing, my pants were still soaked. The snow was just that deep. I slipped off the boots just as we stepped into the mudroom. Then, I took off the scarf, gloves, hat, and jacket Max had loaned me. I hung everything up on the coat rack he had in his mudroom so it could dry.

When I finished, I looked up and found Max watching me. It was clear he had something going through his mind, but he never shared whatever it was. Instead, he urged, "Come on. I'll show you where you'll be sleeping."

I followed behind Max as we climbed the stairs to the second floor of his beautiful home. He took me down the hall to a massive yet gorgeous guest bedroom, where he walked inside and placed my bag down on the end of the bed.

"The guest bathroom is right through that door," he began. "It should have everything you need in there, but if you find something is missing, just let me know."

"I will. Thank you so much."

In the moments that followed, things turned tense. It wasn't necessarily bad, but I had a feeling both Max and I were left wondering where to go next. Thankfully, Max broke the silence.

"I'll get out of your hair so you can change out of those wet clothes and settle in. If you want company, feel free to come and find me. If you need some time to yourself, have at it. No matter what, I want you to be comfortable and to make yourself at home."

I couldn't be certain, but I had a feeling it wouldn't be unwelcome if I hugged him at this juncture. It was so out of character for me; however, Max had been accommodating, kind, and sweet. I felt compelled to express my gratitude. So, I took a step toward him, slid my arms around him, and gave him a hug. "I really appreciate your kindness, Max. Thank you for being so generous and opening your home to me."

Max's body had tensed initially when I hugged him, but within seconds it was gone. His arms came around me, and he returned the hug. His voice sounded a bit husky when he replied, "Any time you need me, Ella…"

At that, he let me go and walked out.

Two minutes later, I was still standing in the space where he left me. Eventually, I snapped out of it and got myself changed. After, I plugged in my phone and fired up my laptop. Once the phone had enough of a charge, I turned it on and set up a wireless hotspot. I needed to check-in and make sure all was running smoothly with work. Most importantly, I needed to reach out to my two best friends so I could get their advice about my current situation.

I confirmed there were no major, or even minor, work issues that needed my attention, and moved on to what I'd been dying to do since Max stood at my front door yesterday. I pulled up my messenger program and entered Steph and Maggie, my best friends, as my recipients. Then, I sent them a text.

I'm currently living in the midst of a monster snowstorm here in northern Maine, but you'll be happy to know that I'm messaging you both from the comfort of my neighbor's guest bedroom.

Within seconds, I saw that at least one of them was replying. Sure enough, only moments later, a text came through.

Steph: Wait. You mean the guy you are always watching from your office?

Me: It's not ALWAYS.

Maggie: OMG. You're in his bedroom? How did this happen?

Me: It's not his bedroom. It's the guest bedroom. And I officially became a damsel in distress when the propane tank that powers my generator ran out of gas. The temps are so cold right now and it's only stopped snowing for brief periods of time. He was outside when my generator shut off and came over to offer me a place to stay.

Steph: I'm squealing over here! This is so exciting. What's he like?

Me: He's the sweetest, most compassionate man I've ever met. And I've officially decided I want to marry him.

Steph: Ahh!!! Love!!

Maggie: When do we get to meet him?!?!

Me: Relax, girls. He's been very flirtatious and has used his body to warm me up, but nothing like that has happened.

Steph: Oooh. I remember that pic you sent of him. He's got an amazing body. I bet it was nice being warmed up by him.

I rolled my eyes and laughed. I forgot that I'd sent the girls a picture I'd taken of Max from my office one day not long after I'd arrived in Maine. He was outside doing some landscaping, and I was busy ogling him. I didn't think it was fair for me to keep the identity of my future husband from my best friends, so I offered up some eye candy. They weren't disappointed.

Returning my attention back to the conversation, I sent another message.

Me: I'm really worried.

Maggie: What?! Why?

Me: Because it's only been a day and I really like him. But it's not just that. This man is the kind of man I know I could easily fall in love with. We get along really well, and it's clear there's an attraction on both sides, but I'm worried he'll be turned off once he finds out who I am.

Steph: Maybe he won't.

Maggie: Yeah, maybe he'll find you even sexier than you already are.

Me: That NEVER happens.

Steph: First time for everything.

Me: I'll believe it when I see it.

Maggie: You've got to give him a chance to prove it to you.

Me: I should get going now. I've got to get myself unpacked and settled.

Maggie: Unpacking…nice. Sounds like something you do when there's an extended stay.

Steph: Haha. So true! You better keep us in the loop. We want regular updates.

Me: Yeah, yeah. You're both crazy. I'll talk to you later.

Steph: Love you, Ella.

Maggie: XOXO

Me: Same.

I closed my laptop and disconnected the hotspot on my phone. Then, I hopped out of bed and started unpacking my things. As I put my clothes in the dresser and my toiletries in the bathroom, I thought about my conversation with my two best friends.

Maybe Steph was right. Maybe there was a first time for everything. I didn't know where things were headed with Max and me. While there was no denying the innuendo in a lot of what he said, I wasn't entirely sure he was interested in something serious.

But I knew that I wanted that with someone. And I believed Max could very well be that someone for me. I wanted a chance at love with a man like him. One who was as handsome as him. One who looked out for me. And one who teased me and made me laugh more in less than twenty-four hours than I'd done since I'd moved to Maine three months ago.

Yes, I definitely wanted a man like Max.

In fact, I wanted to make him *my* old man.

CHAPTER 5

Eleanor

WHEN MY EYES FLUTTERED OPEN THE NEXT MORNING, IT took me a few seconds to remember where I was. But the moment it all came flooding back, I felt myself smile. Because even though yesterday started off horribly, it quickly turned around and had truly been one of the best days of my life. And that was all thanks to Max.

Max, who apparently carried my sleeping self to bed last night.

Following my chat with my friends yesterday and the subsequent unpacking that I did, I spent the rest of the day mostly with my new temporary roommate. We had both lunch and dinner together. Just before dinner, I took a shower. Otherwise, I watched television for a bit while Max took off somewhere in the house. When he returned, he joined me. We talked for some time about inconsequential things. Our conversation was easy and comfortable, and I never felt any pressure to find something to talk about. We either did or didn't. And it was great both ways.

But because of the lack of sleep from the previous night, I was exhausted. I felt myself drifting in my spot on the couch in front of the television. That was the last thing I remembered, which led me to the conclusion I made just a few moments ago about how I'd ended up in the guest bedroom knowing I didn't walk here myself.

I let my day with Max filter through my brain for a couple more minutes before I decided it was time to get up and get moving. After taking care of business in the bathroom and throwing on a pair of leggings and a cute top, I made my way downstairs.

I was surprised to see that Max wasn't in the kitchen. Initially, I thought he might still be sleeping, but I saw a glass in the sink that wasn't there last night. So, once I poured myself a cup of coffee, I went in search of him.

Normally, I'd have been hesitant roaming around someone's house; however, I'd been given specific instructions by the owner himself to make myself at home. I figured it wouldn't hurt to find Max so I could say 'good morning' to him.

Max's home was, much like mine, very large. But where mine had lots of modern, contemporary upgrades, Max's didn't. In fact, it seemed that his home had what I could only assume were custom upgrades. And it struck me then that while some of the upgrades were something that added to the home's aesthetic, most of them were uniquely-made practical upgrades.

I was just about to pass by a closed door when I heard a sound that I assumed could only be coming from Max. I knocked gently, but there was no answer. Listening closely, I confirmed that he was, in fact, behind the door. But he sounded far away, and I had no idea what he was doing. There were noises coming from him that made me think he might be hurt.

Once I heard him let out what sounded like another grunt of pain, I decided it was best to go in. Opening the door, I found that I'd located his basement. Other than a flight of steps, there was no longer a barrier between the sounds coming from Max and my ears.

I descended the stairs quickly, gravely concerned about him. But when he came into view, I realized I shouldn't have gone searching for him.

Because now I was standing there, holding a cup of coffee in my hand, staring at a half-naked Max. His back was to me. I should have turned around and gone right back up the stairs. But I didn't. I couldn't peel my eyes away from the sight of him before me.

He was working out.

He was wearing a pair of black gym shorts and nothing else.

His body was large.

Solid.

So incredibly gorgeous.

Max was, without question, the most beautiful man I'd ever seen in my life.

And with each punch he landed on the punching bag, I marveled at the sheer power behind them. My eyes were riveted to the wide frame of his upper body, the muscles contracting with each of his movements. I was struggling to catch my breath at the vision of him before me.

It wasn't until I realized I was no longer looking at Max's back, but his front instead, that I snapped out of it. Of course, I gave myself a very small window of time to truly appreciate his chest and abdomen. Max wasn't super lean and ripped with a six-pack. He was simply... large. Thick. Manly.

I just barely stopped myself from drooling when my eyes left Max's torso and moved to his face. He was giving me a sly grin.

"Good morning, old man," I greeted him.

He let out a laugh and shook his head as he walked over to me with a smile on his face. "Good morning, Ella."

His voice. My God. His voice saying my name like that first thing in the morning was everything I could have imagined and more. Between that and the scent of him, all sweat and masculine and utterly divine, it was more than my poor senses could handle.

"Did you sleep okay?" he asked.

I found it difficult to speak with a parched throat, but I managed to rasp, "Yeah."

Max didn't respond. He stood there breathing heavy with sweat running down his body.

I needed to do something. Anything. So I said, "I'm assuming you carried me to bed last night. Thank you for making sure I didn't spend the night on the couch."

"Wait. You don't remember me carrying you to bed last night?" he asked.

I shook my head. *"No."* When Max didn't immediately respond, I started to get a little nervous. "What?" I asked. "Why are you looking at me like that?"

Through a full-blown grin, Max shared, "You begged me to take you to my bed."

I gasped. "I did not!"

"You did," he insisted, his tone serious.

I mustered up my most chilling look and replied, "I don't believe you."

Max laughed. "Okay. But you did."

I needed to change topics, so I quickly declared, "Well, I wanted to do something to show my appreciation for everything you're doing for me, so I was going to ask you if you'd like me to make breakfast this morning. But now I'm reconsidering it."

He shrugged and began walking past me toward the stairs. "That's alright. I'm going to go grab a shower now. When I'm done, I can make my own breakfast. I'm feeling like some eggs and bacon today. And I'll even be nice and make some for you, too."

As Max climbed the stairs ahead of me, I wanted to growl my frustration at him. But I didn't. Instead, I just watched him.

What could I say? He had a fantastic backside.

While Max showered, I made bacon and eggs. It was thirty minutes after our standoff in the basement when

Max and I were sitting down to eat breakfast. I'd just shared how amazed I was at the sheer amount of snow that was outside. The worst of the storm was over, but we were still expected to get another two or three inches of accumulation throughout the day. Max told me that he planned to go out early the next morning to start plowing the driveways.

"Driveways?" I questioned him with a piece of bacon held between my fingers.

"Some of the neighbors," he explained after swallowing a forkful of eggs. "Everybody gets out and does what they can with their snow blowers. But I've got a plow, as does one other neighbor. So, we try to help out."

I liked hearing that. Even though Max had irrevocably proven just how compassionate he was by allowing me to stay with him, hearing him share that I'd essentially moved into a community where the people cared about one another like that warmed my heart.

"It's such a great group of people who live here," I felt compelled to share.

Max let out a laugh and warned, "You might rethink that after I tell you about the conversation I had with Walt earlier this morning."

My brows pulled together. I couldn't imagine what Walt would have said that would make me think ill of him. He was such a sweet man. "What did he say?" I wondered.

"He might be older, but Walt's a tough, capable guy," Max began. "Even still, I like to check in on him and Betty for my own peace of mind. I called over there this morning to make sure they were doing okay. Walt insisted I should be calling to check on you instead of him. That's when I shared that you were staying here with me."

Uh oh. I braced for whatever Max was going to share next.

"Walt didn't even respond to me. He shouted out to Betty and told her. That woman was over the moon when she heard."

I dropped my head back and looked to the ceiling. "So now they're going to think something is going on between us," I surmised.

"Yep," Max agreed with a big, beaming smile on his face.

I returned my gaze to him and found he didn't seem the least bit bothered by that fact. When I cocked an eyebrow at him, he just laughed at me. Not surprisingly, I found myself needing to switch gears once again and find something else to talk about.

"So, the whole state is essentially shut down right now?" I asked.

"Pretty much, especially up here in the northern part. All the businesses are basically closed until further notice, which likely won't be until the power is back. But the coastal towns weren't hit nearly as hard, so they'll be back up and running before we are," he explained, seemingly unbothered by the fact that I'd led the discussion elsewhere.

"And when will you have to go back to work?" I pressed.

"Probably not for another month," he said as though he were guessing.

I shook my head in disbelief. "Another month? Where do you work?"

Smiling at me, Max asked, "Have you ever heard of King Enterprises?"

"No," I answered.

"Family business. Contracting and construction. It's the largest in Maine and in the highest demand. My great-grandfather started it years ago. His son, my dad's dad, took it over from him. He had two sons, my dad and my uncle, who took it over from him. And now, I own it with my cousin."

Worried that I'd possibly brought up painful memories, my voice was soft when I stammered, "Your dad... is he still—"

"He's alive," Max cut me off and eased my worries. "But it's a physically demanding job, and he's getting older. It's always been something he loves to do, so he still shows up at job sites, but he's out of it in the official sense. He and my mom are enjoying their golden years. And they deserve that because he worked hard to provide for us, while my mom worked hard to raise her family."

"Do you have any siblings?" I asked.

"An older sister named Courtney," he shared.

"She's not in the family business?" I guessed.

Max shook his head. "No. She didn't want to be involved with it. Dad gave her the option, and she decided against it. When our parents pass, she'll get a larger share of the inheritance so it all equals out in the end."

Something dawned on me then. "Did you build this house?" I wondered.

"I bought the house that was here, demolished it, and rebuilt the entire thing."

I looked around the house at all of the intricate, yet gorgeous details. "It's really beautiful," I praised him.

"Thank you," he replied. "It was a lot of work, but I don't regret any of it."

The minute I got some time alone I was going to open my laptop and research King Enterprises. I wanted to know more about Max but didn't want to start a conversation that would likely lead to him asking about my work again.

"So, how do you plan to spend your day today, old man?"

Max's voice was low when he leaned toward me and returned, "I haven't quite figured that out yet, darling."

Gosh, I seriously loved hearing him call me that.

I put my elbow up on the counter, rested my chin in my hand, and asked, "Care to play a game?"

Looking intrigued, Max replied with a devilishly handsome grin, "Absolutely."

For the next several hours, Max and I laughed our asses off while we played Catchphrase: Uncensored. He thought it was great, mostly because I seemed to be the one who kept getting all of the naughty words. He'd know it, too, because apparently I blushed every single time. It eventually got to a point where he started calling out random, inappropriate words in an effort to save me from my embarrassment. It was the most I'd laughed in a very long time, and even though I didn't share it with him, I couldn't have been more grateful to Max for giving that to me.

After we had lunch, I asked Max if he'd mind me using his gym to get a workout in. I didn't work out nearly as often as I probably should have, but there was entirely too much sexual tension between us. I was afraid if I didn't do something to release some of it, I'd combust. Max, in true Max fashion, had no problem with me using his gym equipment.

Following my workout, which did little to help the ache between my legs, I ran up to the guest bathroom and showered. It was still too early for dinner by the time I finished, so I got on my computer and worked for a bit. I had some emails to deal with and a few tech-related issues to handle. One of my apps was my meal ticket and required regular monitoring. I found that if I set aside a little bit of time every day, I was able to manage it well. I had one other app that was nearly as successful, so I put just as much effort into that one as well. While I had a handful of other apps that I'd developed that did well, they weren't essential to my survival. So, I took on tasks for those as I had the time. Generally, any issues with those weren't nearly as pressing. Thankfully, there weren't any tasks that were overly daunting that I needed to tend to for any of my apps today, so I was able to get my work done relatively quickly.

By the time I descended the stairs again, I found Max already in the kitchen making dinner. "You should have called up to me," I claimed. "I would have come down and helped you prepare everything."

"It's alright. I've got it tonight," he assured me. "You can take charge tomorrow considering I'll be out all day handling the snow removal."

"That works for me. What's for dinner?" I asked.

"Chicken and cheese quesadillas."

"Sounds fantastic."

Twenty minutes later, Max held a plate out to me and ordered, "Couch."

"What?" I asked, taking the plate from him.

"Dinner and a movie," he explained.

I had no doubt I was going to cry. While I knew it was just because we were stuck inside and Max was who he was, I was overwhelmed with joy at the thought of what felt like a real date with him.

Maybe I was crazy for looking at this like it was a date, especially considering Max hadn't indicated it was anything more than just a friendly dinner with the neighbor he was helping. But I couldn't help myself because this was my idea of a perfect date. I didn't need the fancy dinners out at a restaurant or flowers before he picked me up to take me somewhere special. This was all I needed. The company of a great man. If good food was part of the equation, that made it even better.

Doing my best to swallow past the lump in my throat, I followed Max into the great room.

He set his plate down and snatched the remote off the coffee table as he sat down right next to me. No sooner did he open the menu on the television when I saw where he was headed. My body got tight as I started to panic. Max noticed, stopped what he was doing, and called, "Ella?"

"Hmm?"

"Are you okay?" he asked.

I tried my best to appear calm and collected when I responded, "What? Yeah, I'm fine."

"Are you sure?" he pressed.

I gave him a nod.

I didn't know if he believed me, but he redirected his attention to the television once again. He did it speaking. "Do you have a preference for a movie?"

Shaking my head, I said, "Not really. Horror isn't exactly my thing, but I'll watch just about anything else."

Max scrolled through a few movies, but ultimately decided on a great one: *Ocean's Eleven*.

"Have you seen this before?" he asked.

I smiled and replied, "I love it."

Satisfied with my answer, he swapped out the remote for his plate and crossed his legs at the ankles on the table. I took a cue from him and did the same. Then, we settled in and ate dinner while we watched a great movie.

I didn't know if it was because I'd gotten so into the movie or not, but roughly ten minutes after I set my empty plate on the coffee table, I was caught off guard. Max threw his arm behind my head and his hand landed on my opposite shoulder. He didn't hesitate to curl me into his body. My hand flew to his abdomen.

"Max," I hesitated, looking up at him. "Um, what—"

"Relax, darling," he urged, his voice gentle. His eyes remained focused on the television.

When he said it like that, I couldn't not relax. Besides, it wasn't like I didn't enjoy being that close to him. We continued to watch the movie, and everything was great. But, once again, I was thrown when right before the heist actually started, Max shifted us on the couch. The next thing I knew, I was laying down in front of Max, the front of his body pressed into the back of mine. His hand was draped over my hip.

I loved everything about the way it felt.

So, I didn't move. I didn't try to protest. I didn't say anything. I simply enjoyed being there, with him, watching a movie.

And in the end, when Danny Ocean won back his ex-wife, Tess, I rolled to my back and looked up at Max.

"He got her back," I stated.

Max's eyes searched my face briefly before he asserted in a low tone, "You're so beautiful."

My lips parted in shock. I hadn't expect his response.

"I really want to kiss you, Ella," he went on. "I've wanted to kiss you since I showed up on your doorstep two days ago."

I didn't know what I was thinking when I instantly blurted, "I've wanted to do a lot more than just kiss you ever since I saw you outside your house working on it a month after I moved in next door."

With that statement, Max dropped his head and crushed his mouth to mine.

Apparently, Max was thinking similar thoughts to mine earlier. This was a first real date for us.

And evidently, we both kissed on the first date.

CHAPTER 6

Eleanor

MAX WAS AN EXTRAORDINARY KISSER.

The instant his lips touched mine and his tongue swept into my mouth, I felt something come over me. Kissing him was like nothing I'd ever experienced with anyone else. I knew that was special. It had to be something more than just first-date excitement.

I truly hoped it was the start of something incredible. I wanted it to be the beginning of a chance at a real relationship. A chance at love. For me, Max was the total package. He was handsome. So very handsome. He was kind and compassionate. Evidently, he was the best kisser in the world. But most of all, he made me laugh. Nobody had ever made me laugh the way Max did.

So even though we hadn't yet taken things all the way, I didn't care. Sex was important. Of course it was. But even if it ended up not being all that great with Max—which I didn't think was going to be possible anyway—it wouldn't matter. Because being able to laugh with him the way that I did brought me fulfillment I didn't know I needed.

"Ella," he whispered against my mouth.

And the way he said my name. That was *everything*.

Max was on top of me, his hips settled between my parted thighs, and I could feel how hard he was for me. I felt like I had wanted him so badly for so long, and I was finally going to get my wish. I was going to get him.

"Max," I moaned. The need in my voice was unmistakable as I ran my hands through his thick, black hair.

He trailed his lips down my throat, mostly kissing but occasionally nipping the skin along the way. One of his hands was running up and down the side of my body from my thigh, up along my hip, until it reached my breast. He hadn't yet touched me there. His hand made it to right where his thumb would just barely brush the underside of my breast before he'd move it away and back down my side.

"Please," I begged.

"What, darling?" he asked when he'd brought his mouth to my ear. "What do you need?"

"You, Max. Please, I want you."

He emitted a deep growl from the back of his throat as he lifted himself from my body and stood. Max took me with him, and the next thing I knew, we were living out his preferred method of travel with us being chest to chest. My legs were wrapped tightly around his waist as Max, with his hands on my bottom, carried me through the house toward the stairs. While he climbed the steps, I removed my shirt. By the time he made it to the second floor, my bra was gone.

With lightning-fast speed, Max had made it to his room and tossed me onto the bed. He stood beside it as he quickly stripped out of his clothes. I shoved my hands in my pants at my hips and pushed my bottoms off.

"Fuck, look at you, Ella," he muttered. "Naked and gorgeous in the middle of my bed."

With expert-like ease, Max rolled on a condom before he settled himself over me. He closed his mouth over my nipple while his fingers slipped through the moisture that had gathered between my legs.

I couldn't stop the moan from escaping. When one of Max's fingers pushed inside me, I cried out at the glorious sensation. Max slid a second finger inside, and I rode them hard. Months of wanting this man's hands on me had me doing everything I could to relieve the ever-growing ache. I desperately needed to find relief from it.

But just when I was on the verge, Max pulled his fingers from my body and rasped, "I want you to come with me inside you, Ella."

"Hurry," I begged.

Max didn't make me wait. Once he was buried inside me, he gave me about a half a second to adjust to his size before he pulled back and drove in harder. One of his hands was planted in the bed just beside my chest. The other hand was cupping my breast, his thumb stroking over my nipple. Every so often, he'd add a second finger and give it a gentle pinch before moving to the other side.

With each solid, deliberate thrust of his cock into

me, Max was attempting to communicate something. I just didn't know what it was. Not until he spoke with a voice so thick with emotion I nearly came on the spot.

"Christ, three months," he muttered. "Three months I missed out on having this with you. Where have you been, Ella?"

It wasn't a question that required an answer. His words had said it all.

Max's pace increased. I worked my hips to match each of his thrusts. And within seconds, I was coming apart calling out his name. Very soon after I'd had my orgasm, Max found his.

A couple minutes later—after we'd both cleaned up and he disposed of the condom—Max and I were tangled up with each other in his bed. It was a place I'd dreamt of being for months, and now I was here, basking in the glory of just how magnificent it had been. It felt a bit surreal.

"Okay, I need to say something," I announced after some silence had stretched between us.

"What is it?" he asked.

"I know I've been joking around with you the past few days, but there is nothing about what you just did that screams old man."

Max rolled from his back to his side toward me. He did it laughing. When most of his laughter had died down, he reminded me, "I told you. And if you give me five minutes to recover, I'll show you that stamina we were talking about yesterday."

"Looking forward to it, big guy."

Max and I stayed like that, happy and comfortable wrapped up in one another. Five minutes later, he showed me just how much stamina he had.

And when he held me close after our second round of lovemaking because that's precisely what it was, I found it took me a little bit to find sleep. I was silently hoping and praying that when Max found out the truth about exactly who I was, he wouldn't go running, taking my heart with him.

I was woken up the next morning by Max gently kissing the skin of my bare shoulder. I moaned because it was morning, I was warm, and Max's lips were touching me. Wanting to tease him, I arched my back, sending my bottom right into his lap.

Max groaned and squeezed my hip. That hand then moved down over my belly and stopped right between my legs. One swipe through and Max learned how turned on I was. I lost his hand and the heat of him pressed against my back. Immediately, I shifted and turned in the bed to find him rolling on another condom.

At that point, it was safe to assume stamina was not an issue for Max.

Once the condom was situated, Max's hand came around me and he urged, "Hop up, darling."

I smiled at the use of words he'd said to me before he carried me back to my house yesterday morning. What I didn't do was delay in accommodating his request for me to hop up.

Just under two hours after I'd been woken up by Max's kisses on my shoulder, he was giving me a kiss on the lips. We'd had our breakfast and coffee together, but now he was going to be heading out for most of the day. He was starting at the beginning by plowing his driveway before heading out to see if any of the neighbors needed his help.

"What are you going to do?" he asked.

"I'm probably going to give my parents a call first," I started. "Then, I'll call my best friends, Steph and Maggie. After that, I'm going to get dinner in the crockpot before I try to get some work done. If I'm feeling good or you aren't back yet, I might throw in a dessert to go with dinner."

Seemingly pleased with my list, Max said, "Good. Stay busy. I'll probably stop in very briefly so I can simply grab a quick bite to eat around lunchtime."

"Okay," I acknowledged. "I'll be sure to be free at lunchtime, even if it's going to be a quick one."

Max smiled at me, gave me one last kiss, and turned to walk out into the cold.

Just as I told Max I would, I got down to business and stayed busy. First up, I changed the order of my list. I got dinner going in the crockpot because I didn't want to think about that again until much later. I had every intention of baking desserts, but had too much in my brain that needed processing. So, I dashed upstairs to the guest bedroom and grabbed my phone. I pulled up my mom's name in my list of recent calls and tapped on it.

"Hi, Nora," my mom greeted me after a few rings.

"Hey. How's it going there?" I returned.

"We're perfectly fine," she answered. "Your dad has been worried about you, though. He told me that I needed to find out how you're doing. He's concerned about your power being out and whether or not the snow has stopped. Is it still snowing or has it stopped? Did your power come back on?"

I loved my parents. Dad would always find a way to get Mom to ask all his pertinent questions that indicated just how much he worried about me. But if he was talking to me himself, he always spoke with such confidence. It was like he never wanted me to think he doubted my capabilities.

"The snow has finally stopped," I began. "But the power is not back on yet. From what I've seen on the news and what I've been told, that's probably still quite a few days away. I think today is going to really be the first day that emergency personnel and road crews are going to be able to get out there and start the cleanup. Apparently, the freezing rain and ice that fell before the snow came is what made this storm as bad as it was. So many trees had fallen before the snow even started."

"Yeah, we've been trying to keep our eyes on the news reports just to see what's going on up there, but you just never know what it's like in a specific place un-less you hear it from someone who is there. All the reports are talking about the bigger cities, so we have no idea what it's like for you," she explained.

"I'll take a few pictures today and send them over to you," I offered. "There's so much snow outside right now. More than I've ever seen in my life. I think they're saying well over forty inches fell, but some spots are really bad because of the snowdrifts."

Excitedly, my mom replied, "Oh, yes! You should definitely send some pictures. Your dad would love to see that."

I had to laugh. I had no doubts my parents would sit there and marvel over the pictures I sent, but would ultimately go around showing all their friends those pictures of the snowstorm their daughter survived. They make me out to be some kind of superhero when the truth was that had it not been for Max I'm not sure I would have made it through this storm alive.

"Since the power isn't back on, are you still staying with your neighbor?" she asked after my laughter had died down.

I took in a deep breath and blew it out before I answered, "Yes, I am. And Mom?"

"Yeah?" she replied, her curiosity evident.

"I think I'm falling in love with him," I revealed.

Silence stretched between us as my mom hesitated to respond. Eventually, she spoke, but there was a bit of trepidation in her tone. "It's only been a few days, Eleanor."

I bit my lip to suppress my laughter. Mom had never been good at hiding anything. Whenever she was deciding whether or not she wanted to lecture me on something, she called me by my full name.

"I know," I assured her. "It's crazy, Mom. So absolutely crazy. But I know what I feel when I'm around him. And I know that has to mean something. Because what I feel reminds me of what you've always told me you felt when you and Dad met. Something about Max just feels different from anyone else I've ever dated. He's the most generous man I've ever met. In fact, he's outside plowing the snow in his driveway, which is even longer than mine, and then he's going to go and assist the neighbors who need help with snow removal as well. He looks out for people and cares about them."

"Okay, honey, those are all great qualities," she admitted. "There's no denying that, but are you sure what you're feeling is love and not just admiration for a good soul? There's a big difference, and I don't want you ending up hurt."

"He makes me laugh," I swooned. "Mom, I laughed for *hours* yesterday. Hours. I can't explain it, but something about this just feels right with him."

There was a beat of silence before she replied, "Then I only have one question for you, Nora. I know how you are, so you know I have to ask. Have you told him the truth about who you are?"

"No," I whispered, my throat tight as I struggled to get the single word out.

I heard her take in a deep breath. "You have to tell

him, honey. If this is what you believe it is, you don't want to start it by keeping secrets."

"But I really like him a lot," I confessed.

"All the more reason you need to tell him," she insisted.

She was right. I knew she was right, but that still didn't mean I wanted to share it and risk what I had with Max. "I'm afraid."

"Of what?"

"Losing him," I admitted. "I know it's early, Mom. But I don't want to lose this feeling. I don't want to lose him."

"If he's who you believe he is, Nora, you won't. But for your sake, please promise me that you're going to tell him. The last thing you want to do is fall even harder for this man, make him fall for you, and then end up in a situation where you're responsible for breaking both of your hearts. With you being so far away, Dad and I already worry about you. If you're that far away with a broken heart, we couldn't stand it."

I didn't respond.

"Nora?" Mom called.

"Yeah?" I answered.

"Promise me," she pleaded.

I hesitated briefly, but ultimately replied, "I promise."

"Before your heart gets involved and you can wind up heartbroken?" she clarified.

Taking in a deep breath, I held it and explained, "It's already too late for that."

There was a collective sigh between us. If Max

turned out not to be the man I thought he was, there was not a doubt in my mind that I'd feel the loss of him. The thought was too painful to bear.

Realizing there wasn't much else to say that would make the task ahead of me any easier, Mom and I shifted our conversation to other topics. We talked for a long time; that was just our way. But with more calls to make to Maggie and Steph, work-related tasks to complete, and dessert to be baked, I had to end our call.

Following my conversation with my mom, I took a break from the phone and pulled out my laptop. As quickly as I could, I got through my emails and solved the one tech-related problem I needed to handle. By that point, it was approaching lunchtime. I went downstairs so I could whip up something for Max when he came in from working out in the cold all morning.

With near-perfect timing, Max walked in the door just as I'd finished preparing the food. What he did next surprised me. Instead of taking a load off and diving in, he came right over to me and gave me a kiss on the lips.

I allowed the good feeling that gave me to sink in for just a moment. Then, I asked, "How's it going out there, old man?"

Max smiled and said, "Believe it or not, I just got my driveway finished. With one of our usual storms and my driveway being so long, it typically takes me a while to clear it. But with the depth of the snow and the drifts we had, it took a lot longer this time."

"Well then, you better eat up so you can get back out there and help your neighbors," I advised him. "If they're trying to do snow removal with shovels or snow blowers, you arriving with a plow will be a miraculous blessing."

With that, Max wasted no time in downing his lunch. He was a man who had things to do, and this was not the time to drag his heels. Before he ventured back outside, Max thanked me for feeding him and gave me another kiss.

And the ease with which he did that melted my heart. I wanted something that simple and meaningful for the rest of my life. Just the simplicity of a passing kiss from Max while I stood at the kitchen counter preparing to bake dessert. I wanted that without the truth being withheld. I longed to find a man like Max for what seemed like forever. I just hoped when I gave him the truth, I'd be able to still have him and my successful professional life.

CHAPTER 7

Eleanor

I was in Max's bedroom, standing at the window that had a clear view to my house. My mind was whirling with a million thoughts about what to do.

After Max went back out to help the neighbors following lunch, I prepared dessert for after dinner tonight. Then, I called Steph and Maggie. Even though I'd already told my mom about Max and valued her opinion, I had promised my friends that I'd keep them updated.

Of course, they were thrilled to hear about how things had progressed between Max and me. But like my mom, they both urged me to be forthcoming with him insisting that it was not only something he deserved, but that I did as well.

I got it. In any other situation, I knew I'd never hide anything from Max...or any other partner for that matter. But this one thing seemed to be such a source of contention for me. The minute a man learned of my success, he communicated less and less until, eventually, I stopped hearing from him altogether. Up until now, nobody I'd spent my time with made me feel the way Max did. The fact that he could possibly respond to the news the same way everyone else did was my sole reason for not sharing. I wasn't ready to let him go.

Even still, I knew my mom, Steph, and Maggie were right. Max deserved the truth. More than that, I really didn't need to get myself in deeper with someone who might not be able to stick it out with me because of pride or ego. There wasn't a doubt in my mind that I deserved better than that.

But it was hard. Because even though I knew what I deserved, it didn't make it any easier to come to terms with the fact that I might lose Max as a result. So, I was struggling with trying to figure out the best way to share the news with him.

As I stood there staring out the window while contemplating my options, something caught my eye. That's when I noticed Max's truck was in my driveway. He was plowing it for me. Seeing that did two things to me. First, it made me fall harder for him. I mean, the guy had been out all day, and he was taking the time to do my driveway as well. Second, I suddenly had the overwhelming urge to do something to help him. I looked out one of the other windows and saw just how I could do that.

So as quickly as I could, I got myself layered up and bundled up. Then, I sauntered out to Max's garage. I found a shovel and a snow blower. Being from Florida, I hadn't ever used a snow blower before. Given my lack of experience with one, I figured the shovel was the safest bet. Grabbing it off the hook, I walked out to the front walkway that led from the driveway to the front door of his house. It was still completely covered in snow.

I took in a deep breath, blew it out, and got down to business. I speared the snow with the shovel, scooped, and tossed it off to the side. I did it again and again. The snow was heavy, wet, and dense, so it was quite an undertaking. I didn't know how much time had passed, but it felt like it had been hours. This wouldn't have necessarily been a problem; however, I was freezing *and* I'd only managed to get about a third of Max's walkway cleared. The snow was so deep that it took several shovelfuls of snow just to clear one small section. When I took that into consideration, I actually felt pretty proud of myself.

With a renewed sense of determination, I rammed the shovel into the huge pile in front of me and continued my task. It couldn't have been more than another twenty minutes later when I finally heard and saw Max's truck barreling up his driveway. I smiled and waved at him before getting back to the task at hand.

Part of me was proud of myself for getting as much of the walkway cleared as I did, but the other part of me was disappointed that I'd only gotten just under half of it cleared. I had really been hoping I would have been able to surprise Max.

I was mid-scoop when Max growled, "What the hell are you doing?"

I froze on the spot and felt my body get tight. Evidently, Max was angry.

Why was he angry?

Slowly, I turned around and looked up at him. "Excuse me?" I asked.

"Why are you out here shoveling snow?" he wondered.

If anyone else had asked that question, it might seem inquisitive. But when Max asked it with the look on his face and his voice as low and angry as it was, that question was a far cry from curious.

"I was...you," I stammered. "I wanted to help."

"Help?" he repeated.

I gave him a nod.

"Ella, I have a snow blower in my garage that'll do this walkway in no time at all. Fifteen, twenty minutes tops," he shared.

My eyes widened. I was certain I'd been out for more than two hours.

Max persisted, "Based on that look on your face and the color of both your nose and cheeks, I'm guessing I wouldn't be wrong to assume you've been out here significantly longer than that."

"Well, yes, but I didn't exactly know how to use the snow blower," I explained, shifting back and forth on my feet. "So, I just thought it would be better to use the shovel."

Max shook his head as he corrected me, "No, darling. It would have been better for you to stay inside where it's warm and left this for me to take care of when I finished the driveways."

"But I saw you," I tried reasoning.

"You saw me?" he asked.

Nodding, I clarified, "I was upstairs in your bedroom looking out the window. I saw you plowing my driveway, and that made me feel all warm inside. Knowing that you were out here, working hard all day, and yet you still wanted to do that for me. I just wanted to do something to show you how much I appreciate everything you've done for me over the last few days."

Something changed in Max's expression. He took the shovel out of my hand, placed his opposite hand in mine, and started walking back toward the open garage door. Once inside, he threw the shovel off to the side. As it clattered to the ground, Max led me back into the house.

I was so caught off guard, I wasn't sure how to respond.

So I didn't.

Max took his gloves off first. Next went his hat, jacket, and finally, his boots.

I didn't move. I just stood there watching him, mostly in shock at this completely new side to him. I hadn't seen him act so peculiar before now.

Having removed his stuff, he came over and stood in front of me. He yanked off my hat, unwrapped my scarf, pulled off my gloves, and removed my jacket.

"Kick off the boots," he ordered.

"Max—" I got out before I took in the change in his face. It was evident that Max was not interested in having a chat.

Unsure about his mood, I decided it was best to kick off my boots and save the questions for later. So, that's what I did.

Without a word, Max slipped his fingers through mine and escorted me through the house and upstairs to his bedroom. He moved through it to the master bathroom where he turned on the shower. It was only then when he gave me another order.

"Time to warm up, Ella," he started. "Strip, darling."

I blinked in surprise, about to say something, though I wasn't sure what, when Max began stripping. Seeing that, I knew it would have been useless for me to put up a fight because, truthfully, I was excited about the prospect of warming up in the shower with him.

So, I did the only thing I could do.

I stripped.

Max smirked and urged me into the shower ahead of him. The minute we stepped under one of the sprays in the dual spray shower, Max turned me in his arms, cupped my breast, and kissed me.

He was already hard between us. With his tongue in my mouth and his thumb gliding over my nipple, I couldn't help myself. I wrapped my fingers around his length and stroked. Max groaned into my mouth.

Hearing that sent a shot of desire right between my legs. As if sensing it, Max slid his hand down my abdomen until it landed right between my legs. He rubbed me there gently before slipping a finger inside. Max alternated between plunging his fingers inside me and tenderly rubbing me. The change in pressure was indescribable.

For a while, I managed to continue stroking him and kissing him, but it eventually became too much.

He'd done such a stellar job working me up, I was on the brink of an orgasm. My mouth disconnected from his as I moaned. I lost purchase on his cock the closer I got.

Max worked me harder and my breathing grew shallow.

"That's it, Ella," he encouraged me gently. "Let me take care of you."

"Oh, Max," I groaned as my orgasm took over, sending pleasure through my body. My legs gave out, but Max's arm was planted firmly around my back and stopped me from falling to the floor.

When I'd come down from the high, Max curled my body into his. I took a minute to stand there under the spray with my body pressed against Max's doing nothing but allowing the feelings I had run through me.

Without any forethought, I began touching my mouth to the skin of Max's chest. My hands began roaming over his body, ultimately finding his cock again. I squeezed and stroked as I continued to kiss him. When I finally tipped my head back and gazed up at him, the look in his eyes was like nothing I'd ever seen before.

Intense was the only way to describe it.

I worked his length harder as one of Max's hands came around to squeeze my ass. He dropped his mouth to mine and kissed me. And not long after, I swallowed the groan he let out when he finally came in my hand.

After a bit more touching and kissing, Max and I finished up in the shower. We did this all without saying anything to one another. Even with the silence, I didn't feel any worry or concern over the situation between us even though Max had been so angry when he found me shoveling the walkway. Despite my belief that everything between Max and me was okay, I still hoped we'd have an opportunity to talk about what happened outside because I didn't quite understand what caused his mood swing.

Once I'd dried myself off and wrapped a towel around my body, I started walking toward the bedroom door.

"Ella?" Max called.

"Yeah?" I answered.

"Where are you going?" Max asked.

Turning back to look at him, I replied, "My clothes are in the guest room."

With a nod of understanding, he stressed, "I'd like to talk to you a minute. Can you come back after you get your clothes?"

"Sure," I said softly.

I hurried down the hall to the guest bedroom and quickly threw on some clothes. Before I went back to Max's room, I took a few deep, settling breaths. I wasn't sure they helped to calm me in the least. By the time I made it back to his room, I found Max lying down in bed wearing nothing but a pair of grey sweats. He held his hand out, urging me to join him.

I placed my small hand in his large one, and he effortlessly tugged me into the bed. I was on my back beside Max, while he was on his side with his head propped up in his hand.

"I think I made it clear that we live in a tight-knit

community here," he began. "I told you I help out my neighbors. It's just the way I am."

Was he saying he plowed my driveway because he was just being a good neighbor?

"Okay?" I responded because I wasn't sure I understood what he was trying to tell me.

"But me plowing your driveway today had nothing to do with me helping out a neighbor," he clarified. "I was doing that because you're my woman now, and it snowed. Your driveway was covered, and it needed to be plowed. As your man, that's my job."

He was my man.

Max King was *my* man.

I tried not to act like a goof given how giddy hearing him say that made me feel, so I remarked, "I can understand that. But I also really appreciated what you were doing for me. I just wanted to do something nice for you in return to show my gratitude."

"Ella, darling, please listen to me," he pleaded. "You don't need to show your thanks for everything I do for you. I suspect if things continue between us like they are, I'm going to find myself in a position where I'll want to do a lot of things for you. It's just the way it's going to be. And that's okay. I don't want you going out of your way to do something for me because you're trying to balance the scales. They don't always have to be balanced."

My brows pulled together. While part of what he said was wonderful, I wasn't sure I liked what all of it seemed to indicate. "This doesn't seem fair. Are you saying that I'm not allowed to do something nice for you?"

"Not at all," he assured me. "What I am saying is that you don't need to do something for me because you feel like you owe it to me. I have no doubts that there will eventually come a time when you will have something you'll want to do for me simply because you just want to do it. And if you're doing it for the same reason I went over and plowed your driveway today, you aren't going to want me to do something else to show you my appreciation because I'm trying to make us even. Because if I do that, it makes what you've done not nearly as special as it could be or should be. I wouldn't want to take that away from you, and I'd like it if you wouldn't try to take it from me. You'll get your turn to tip the scales in your favor, Ella. Trust me."

"Okay, so can I ask a question?" I wondered.

Max dipped his chin.

"You said that if things continued between us like they are now…" I trailed off. "I'm curious how things are between us."

Max seemed genuinely surprised when he asked, "You don't know?"

I bit my lip before I assured him, "I mean, I know how I feel, but we haven't exactly communicated those feelings to one another."

Now, he went from looking surprised to looking confused. "You don't think we've communicated how we feel about each other?"

I rolled my eyes. "I didn't mean like that."

"I know you didn't," he insisted. "But doesn't that tell you something? Darling, we've got great chemistry.

I can't remember a time in my life where I laughed as long and as hard with anyone else the way that I did with you yesterday. Beyond that, you're a little spitfire. You have these moments where you're incredibly soft and sweet that I find endearing. But you also have no problem going toe-to-toe with me and teasing, which only makes me want to take your clothes off and get you in bed. And even though I've trudged through the snow six times for your ass already and even had to carry you a couple of those times, everything with you has been effortless. It's just easy. I really like the idea of easy."

He paused a moment, barely giving me a chance to let all of that sink in. Then, he continued, "From what I can tell so far, you aren't high maintenance and you won't be the kind of woman who will bust my balls over stupid little things. So, it's all of that, plus you've got an amazing body, an unbelievably gorgeous face, and you've been wanting me for the last three months. I'm not sure how I couldn't like what I've got lying in my bed right now."

He just said that.

And every single word he said about me could have been said about him. So, I did the only thing I could and responded, "I feel exactly the same way about you." My throat got tight, but I pushed past it and added, "Except, I didn't trek through the snow for you, and you didn't stare out your window wanting me for the last three months either."

Max grinned when he replied in a low, serious tone,

"Oh yes I did. I've been wanting you for a long time. I just didn't know you were living right next door to me."

He had to stop.

"Stop," I ordered. "I'm going to cry, Max. You can't say things like that."

Max pressed a sweet kiss to my cheek and acquiesced, "Alright, I'll stop."

"Thank you. Now, can I feed you dinner and dessert?" I wondered.

"Dessert?"

Smiling, I nodded and shot back, "You didn't think I was going to let *my* man go outside and work all day without making sure he was going to have something sweet waiting for him after I filled his belly with a hearty meal, did you?"

Max gave me a squeeze in response.

Then, we peeled ourselves out of the bed and went downstairs for dinner and dessert.

CHAPTER 8

Eleanor

I ROLLED TO THE SIDE AND WHIMPERED IN PAIN. EACH muscle fiber in my back and arms felt like it had been through a food processor.

No sooner did I get to my side when I felt Max's body curl up behind mine. He put a hand on my arm, kissed the skin of my shoulder, and asked, "What's the matter?"

Just the thought of moving my body caused me to feel pain. I answered, "Ugh, my body hurts so bad. Why do my back and arms feel so awful?"

Max gently squeezed my arm.

I groaned.

"This is what happens when you go out and try to shovel a walkway of that size with the amount of snow that was on it," Max explained.

"Well, if it upset you yesterday that I went out to do that, this is just a heads up that you won't ever have to worry about me doing that again," I mumbled. "I've never felt this bad in my life."

Max gave me another kiss, this one on the neck just below my ear, before he encouraged gently, "Roll to your belly, darling."

It took superhuman effort, but I managed to make it to my belly. I heard Max exit the bed, and I would have asked him where he was going, but I just didn't have the strength. Luckily, he wasn't gone long and returned not even a minute later.

The next thing I knew, Max was settling himself on my bottom. Within seconds, I heard him rubbing his hands against one another before they touched the skin on my sore back. As he worked his fingers into my muscles, I realized he'd gone into the bathroom and gotten one of my bottles of lotion. His hands were gliding effortlessly over my nearly naked body.

I was so sore that I couldn't quite figure out if I was feeling pleasure or pain from Max's massage. He was doing whatever he could to keep me comfortable. Each time he moved to a new spot, he started with gentle pressure before gradually increasing it.

"Max, I'm convinced I'm going to be utterly useless today," I warned him. "I wasn't joking when I said I've never been this sore before. And not that I don't appreciate what you're trying to do right now, but I'm not convinced it's actually helping me."

"It's helping," he assured me. "You've got to be patient. I'm not a miracle worker."

"You mean, you don't offer instant gratification as part of your services?" I teased.

Max's hands moved from the spot between my

shoulder blades up and out to my shoulders. Then, I felt his chest against my back and his mouth at my ear. With his fingers still massaging my sore muscles, he whispered, "If you behave and stop giving me grief, Ella, I'll finish your arms, and then I'll show you how instantly I can make you feel good."

At his promise, I felt a rush of excitement between my legs. I also felt Max press his hips into my backside. He was hard, clearly ready to do just as he said. I decided it was wise to behave and stop giving him grief.

A few minutes later, Max finished my arms, pulled my panties down my legs, and slid himself through the wetness that had gathered. Then, he was inside me giving me instant gratification.

Roughly twenty minutes after Max had his way with me—when we were still tangled up in each other in his bed—my cell phone rang. I let out a groan of protest but rolled out of the warm and comforting embrace of Max's arms toward the nightstand. It was a local number, but not one I recognized.

"Hello?" I answered.

"Hi, can I speak with Eleanor Page?" a woman asked.

"This is she," I responded.

"Hi, Eleanor. I'm Marie with Gordon's Fueling Service. We apologize for the delay in returning your voice message, but today's the first day we've been able to get back into the office since the storm hit. Anyway, I wanted to let you know that we're able to get out to your place later this afternoon to refill your tank. And due to the circumstances, if the tank needs to be purged because it got too low, we'll waive the fee for that. Are you going to be available this afternoon?"

"Yes, I will be," I confirmed. "What time should I expect you?"

"I don't have a definitive time, but it'll be sometime between one and four," she said. "Will that work for you?"

"Sure. Thank you. Would the driver be able to call me when he's on his way? I'm staying at my neighbor's house since my tank ran out shortly after the storm started, and it was just too cold to stay there without any heat."

"Yes, I'll make a note for your driver to call you when he's on his way to your place," she confirmed. "We'll see you this afternoon then."

"Thanks, Marie."

I disconnected the call and something instantly hit me.

Dropping to my back, I looked at Max and asked, "How is your generator still running?"

"What?" he answered with a question.

"The power has been out for days now," I started. "I thought a tank would have needed to be refilled at this point. Why hasn't yours run out yet?"

Max brought a hand up to gently trace the skin along my collarbone. I loved the delicate, sweet, and tender touch from him, especially when it was the complete opposite of what I'd always expected he'd be like given his size. Anytime he was like that with me, it always surprised me. Despite the fact that I felt slightly bewildered by just how gentle he could be, it didn't change the fact that I absolutely loved that about him.

As he watched his fingers trace over my skin, he remarked, "I told you I rebuilt this place. When I did, I was smart about it. It took some extra time and a lot of extra money, but I plan to be here for the rest of my life. I know how bad the winters in northern Maine can be, and I'm not one who likes being unprepared. So, during the rebuild, I had an oversized underground propane tank put in. If I needed it to, a full tank would give me about a month of power."

My eyes widened in surprise. This was just another one of those practical things that Max had done in his home that most people would never think to do. "That was very smart of you," I praised him.

"I knew that at the time I did it," he began. "But these past few days have reminded me of just how great of an idea it really was."

With the softness of his voice and the feather-light touch of his fingers, I couldn't help but feel all warm and fuzzy inside.

I loved this. I loved having this with him.

And when I realized that, it hit me what was ahead. The gas company was going to be filling my propane tank today. My house would have power once again. My time with Max was about to come to an end, and that thought made me feel incredibly sad.

"Ella?" Max called.

"Hmm?" I replied.

"Why do you suddenly seem so sad?" he wondered.

My head dropped to the side. "That was the gas company," I murmured. "They're coming out today to refill my tank."

Max slid his hand under my jaw, cupped my cheek that was opposite of him, and urged me to look at him. "You're going to miss this?" he guessed correctly.

My eyes filled with tears as I nodded.

"Ella…" He trailed off, slipping an arm between the bed and me and pulling me close to him for a hug.

Gosh, I was such a baby. Max must have thought I was crazy.

"You don't have to be upset," he insisted. "I'm going to be right here. You can come stay here anytime you want. And I'll stay with you at your place, too. There's only a driveway and some land separating our homes, darling."

I pressed my palms against his chest and peered up at him. "You're right. I'm just being silly."

"It's not silly; it's sweet," he assured me. "Seeing that you feel this much for me means a lot, Ella. Especially because I feel the exact same way about you."

"This is really fast," I rasped the truth.

Giving me a tender squeeze, he stressed, "That doesn't mean it's wrong."

He had a valid argument. And considering the speed of my parents' relationship, I knew that it didn't necessarily matter how quickly things progressed. My parents were a perfect example of a how a union between two people could be quick but still long lasting.

Max's words also rang true for me in another facet of my life. I knew better than anyone else how just because something happened fast didn't mean it was wrong. Because I'd experienced it in my professional life. Everything came together quickly for me, and before I had a chance to process what was happening, my life had completely changed. For the better.

And now that I was thinking about that again, I was stuck wondering how to bring the truth up to Max. I had planned to find a way to tell him about it last night, but then other things happened, Max said a lot of sweet words to me, and I didn't want to ruin the moment between us.

"You look like you're a million miles away," Max's voice broke into my thoughts.

Shaking my head, I insisted, "It's nothing. You're right."

"Are you sure?"

I nodded.

"You ready for some breakfast?" he asked.

"Yeah."

With that, Max and I got up, got dressed, and went downstairs to make breakfast. An hour and a half later, following a delicious pancake breakfast, I was standing in Max's great room looking at pictures. He had gone downstairs to the basement to get in a workout not long after we finished eating.

I was going to go upstairs to check my emails and get some work done, but as I passed by the room, the pictures caught my eye. I'd seen the frames the day we sat and watched *Ocean's Eleven*, but I didn't want to interrupt our movie. Then, I completely forgot to ask him about them.

There were three different frames. The first had a picture of a beautiful woman who bore a striking resemblance to Max. She was pictured with a handsome man who had his arm around her shoulders tucking her to his side. The man was holding an adorable little girl, who couldn't have been more than four or five years old in his other arm. And the woman was cradling a very new baby in her arms. I came to the conclusion that this had to be Max's sister and her family.

In the next frame, there was a picture of Max with the little girl. She looked younger than she did in the picture with her family. Neither Max nor the little girl were looking at the camera. They were both mid-laugh, looking at each other. It was the most beautiful photo I'd ever seen. The look on Max's face was breathtaking.

And in the third frame was another picture of Max. This one had both the little girl and, who I could now see was a sweet newborn boy, presumably her younger brother. In the photo, Max and the little girl were both staring down at the baby boy. They were both seemingly mesmerized by the sight of him. My heart melted seeing Max in these photos with his family.

"That's my Claire," I suddenly heard from behind me. When I turned to look at him, Max added, "My favorite little girl in the whole world."

"Your niece?" I guessed.

Max nodded.

"She's beautiful," I offered a compliment. "And I assume the little guy is your nephew?"

"He's not so little now," Max began. "That picture was taken about ten months ago, right after he was born. His name is Julian."

I loved the way Max's face lit up when he was talking about Claire and Julian. It was evident his niece and nephew were the little lights of his life, and I was hoping I'd be able to see him with them one day.

"How old is Claire?" I asked.

"Four going on fourteen," Max remarked. "I do not envy Courtney or Jim. They're going to have their hands full with that one when she's older."

"Do they live close? Do you see them often?" I questioned him.

Nodding, Max confirmed, "They're about a ten-minute drive from here. I saw them yesterday when I was out plowing. Jim's got a riding mower that has the option to remove the mowing deck and put the snow blower extension on in the winter. It works well, but with this amount of snow, I knew they'd need the help. So, their driveway was the first I did after I had lunch yesterday. I went in for a minute after I finished to see the kids. Claire had watched from the window the entire time I was plowing. When I went inside, she jumped up into my arms and begged me to take her out to play. Obviously, I couldn't do it then because I wanted to get back and help some of the neighbors and get your driveway cleared, but I promised her that I'd come back soon to play, hopefully before we get another storm. She accepted that."

I took a couple steps toward Max. Even though he was sweaty from his workout, I didn't care. I slid my arms around his waist, pressed up on my toes, and kissed him. I loved how much he loved his family and how much it filled him with pride to take care of them.

"Claire sounds like an absolute joy," I declared. "And I'm guessing Julian's probably not far off from that either."

A look of contentment washed over Max before he agreed, "Yeah, they are."

"You said that Courtney doesn't work in the family business," I started. "What does she do?"

"She's a stay-at-home mom now. She was an elementary school teacher, but after Claire was born, her world was turned upside down. Courtney loves being a mom. And while she loved her job, it doesn't bring her greater joy than being home with her babies."

I gave him a nod of understanding. "And Jim?" I asked, curious what he did for a living.

"He's a DEA agent," he answered.

My eyes widened in surprise. "Really?"

Max nodded and asked, "Did you hear about that massive drug bust that happened a couple months ago?"

I shook my head.

"There was a cartel that was running drugs from South America up into the United States and Canada. There were several points of entry across the U.S., but Jim's branch received a tip from one of the agencies in Florida. There was talk of a huge stash coming through White Pine. Jim was the lead agent on that case. He and his team managed to seize just over twenty-five million dollars' worth of cocaine."

"Wow," I marveled. "That's crazy."

Max let out a laugh. "You've got no argument from me on that one. I'll stick to construction."

I could have told him how much I would have preferred to stick to app development, but I didn't want to risk having him ask me about them. I just wasn't ready for what him having that information would bring.

So, after a beat of silence, I asked, "Are you going to shower?"

"Yeah. Do you want to join me?" he tried coaxing me.

I took a minute and pretended I was thinking. "I really should try to get some work done," I noted. "But a shower with you sounds like a great distraction from it all."

"Come on," he urged, taking me by the hand and leading me upstairs.

"Wow, I can't believe how cold it is in here," I said. "It's absolutely freezing."

"We've had sub-zero temps at night. The sun was out today and yesterday, but it's not enough to really warm things up."

Max and I were currently at my house waiting for the gas company to arrive and fill my propane tank. I'd received a call about ten minutes ago, and the driver had let me know he was on his way. So, Max and I bundled up and made our way over. When we walked in, I realized there wasn't much difference between the temperature inside my house compared to what it was outside.

"How long do you think it's going to take to warm this place up?" I wondered, shifting my body closer to Max's as I shivered.

"Long enough that I think you should spend one more night at my place just to be on the safe side."

With my arms crossed over my chest as I leaned into him, I looked up at him and declared, "You like me in your bed, don't you, old man?"

He let out a laugh and asked, "Was there ever really a doubt in your mind about that?"

"I guess not."

Just then, Max and I saw the gas truck backing up my driveway. When it reached the top, the driver climbed out and walked around the back side of the truck. He grabbed a small toolbox and began unraveling the hose.

While the driver worked at the propane tank, Max and I hung out inside. He held me tight in his arms because I couldn't stop shivering. When the shivering got to be too much, he started kissing me. I guess he figured he'd find another way to warm me up. It worked great until we were interrupted by a knock on the front door.

The driver explained that he had to purge the system since the tank was empty, but that they didn't add any extra fees to my bill because the storm had essentially delayed them being able to get out and fill it for me before it went completely empty. I left the driver and Max standing at the door talking while I went to get my purse so I could pay the bill.

After I paid, the driver took off and Max got the generator running again for me. We turned on the heat and left to go back to the warmth of Max's house.

That night, when I was curled up in Max's bed with his body running the length of mine and his arms holding me tight, I thought about what was ahead. Tomorrow, I'd be back in my own bed.

And that thought saddened me.

CHAPTER 9

Eleanor
Two weeks later

"MAGGIE AND I WERE TALKING ABOUT IT, AND WE'RE convinced you're holding out on us," Steph declared.

"I'm not holding out on either of you," I assured her. "It's just been really crazy here for the last couple of weeks."

"But you've been back in your house for nearly two weeks now, and you still haven't told us what's going on with you and Max. We're dying for some news."

Maggie and Steph were my best friends, and I loved them dearly. But they over-exaggerated everything. I'd managed to text back and forth with them over the last couple of weeks, but as I told Steph, things had been a little out of sorts.

"Well, that's why I'm calling and talking to you now," I explained. "Things have mostly gotten back to normal here."

"The new normal," Steph corrected me.

"What?"

"Your normal is whatever it is now, but it's the new normal because this is a normal post-winter storm. This is the new normal that includes Max King."

Even though she couldn't see me, I shook my head in disbelief. This girl. Truthfully, it was a good thing she couldn't see me because I couldn't exactly deny what she was saying anyway. I was living out my new normal. And I was finding that it was not a bad place in which to be living.

"Right, Steph, things have gotten back to the new normal here," I agreed. "Anyway, let's move on. So, you remember how I told you about the propane tank being filled up and Max having me stay at his place one more night?"

"Yeah."

"I did. But when it came time for me to come back home the next day, Max ended up coming over with me. He claimed it was because he knew how sad I was feeling about going home alone, but I think it's because he was feeling exactly the same. So, he stayed here that night, but then we spent the night apart the next night. Since then, I've stayed at his place twice and he's stayed here three times."

Steph wasn't one to beat around the bush. She cut right to the chase and asked, "So is it just great sex and a cuddle buddy you've got?"

"It's definitely great sex, but it's so much more than that. For both of us," I told her.

There was silence while she waited for me to say it.

"I love him, Steph," I admitted.

She still didn't respond.

I took that as my cue to continue, "It scares me how much I love him because even though I'd been staring at this man from my office window for the first three months that I lived here, we've really only just gotten to know one another. It hasn't even been a full month yet," I fretted.

My best friend was quick to offer up sound reasoning. "Ella, babe, aren't your parents the epitome of quick? It wasn't a full month for them either, right?"

Steph was asking questions, but they needed no answer. She was correct. When my parents met each other, it was love at first sight according to them. My mom always talked about it, but I remained skeptical. Because I didn't really believe that it was possible to fall in love with someone like that. Sure, I'll admit I lusted after Max when I first saw him outside his house months ago and joked that I was going to marry him. But I never expected that I'd meet him and actually fall for him. More than that, I never expected he'd fall for me. It seemed I was wrong about a lot of things where Max was concerned.

I didn't have a chance to respond to Steph's question because she pressed for more and hit me with the biggest one yet. "Forget about all that for a minute," she ordered. "Can I assume that in all the settling you've done in the last couple weeks you've at least managed to tell him who you are?"

"You could assume that," I stated.

"And would that make me an ass?" she shot back.

I kept my mouth shut.

My best friend knew what my silence meant. "Ella, you *have* to tell him," she insisted.

I sighed. Then, I did my best to defend myself. "I know, I know. But every time I tell myself that I'm going to do it, something comes up. And then I'm either too scared to tell him or I don't want to ruin the moment."

"You can't keep it a secret forever," she stressed. "And if you truly love this guy, think about him. How's he going to feel when it's months down the road before you've shared it with him?"

I sighed again. Everything she was saying was right, but that didn't seem to matter. Because while I knew that my professional success shouldn't have prevented a man from being with me, past experiences had proven otherwise. As much as I wanted to believe he was different, I didn't know how Max would react, which was precisely the reason why I'd been coming up with excuses.

"It might not come as a surprise to him," I speculated. "I mean, I'm his next-door neighbor. He's got to know what my home cost me. Shouldn't that tell him that I'm well off?"

Steph just laughed. Then, she pointed out, "There's a difference between being well off and being a billionaire, Ella. The sooner you realize it, the better off you'll be."

"You make it sound like it's a bad thing," I mumbled. "I don't want to lose him."

"If he's the right guy, you won't. And if he's like the rest and can't handle it, he's not the guy for you."

I knew that, but it still didn't make it any easier to

accept. Especially when I'd finally found a guy that I would actually be upset about losing.

"I know," I admitted.

"Don't wait any longer, Ella. It's only going to get harder as time goes on," she warned. "Try to think about it from his perspective. I mean, how would you feel if the roles were reversed and Max didn't tell you?"

"While it'd hurt to know that he kept it from me, I wouldn't be upset about the actual news. Someone being wildly successful shouldn't be a reason for them to be un-lovable. Sadly, it never seems to be the problem when the man is well off," I argued.

"You've got a valid argument," she said. "But I still think it's a mistake to hold onto something like this."

Just then, as I was staring out my front window, I saw Max's truck come barreling down the driveway. He was driving like a crazy man.

"Hey, Steph, Max just pulled up. I'm going to go, but I'll give you a call soon."

"Okay. Just remember to think about what I said," she urged.

"I will," I promised.

"Love you!"

"You too!"

I disconnected the call and moved to the front door. The second I opened it I knew something was very, very wrong. The look on Max's face was nothing but pure anguish.

"Max?" I called softly, knowing whatever he was go-ing to say was not going to be good.

Tears filled his eyes. "They've got her," he struggled to get out.

"What? Who?" I asked.

His voice. I'll never forget the strangled sound of his voice when he replied, "Claire. She's gone. Courtney just called me, screaming. She's hysterical. Someone kidnapped Claire."

I gasped. "Oh my God."

"I need to get over there, but I need you. Please. Will you come with me?"

"Of course, Max. Anything," I replied, forcing myself not to break down into tears. I wanted to so badly, though. Because Max's favorite girl in the whole world was missing, and I knew how much that was going to hurt him. I never wanted Max to hurt.

I ran through the house, grabbed my keys and purse, and zipped outside.

Ten minutes later, we pulled up outside what I assumed was Max's sister's house. There were several police cars parked in the driveway and along the road. Max threw the truck into park and jumped out. I was out by the time he made it to my side.

Before we had the chance to even take a step toward the house, we heard a woman wail, "Max!"

My eyes shot in the direction of the pained screamed. Courtney, the woman from the picture in Max's home, was running toward him, her phone in her hand. Her body collided with his and bucked with her uncontrollable sobs. "They've got my baby! We've got to get her back, Max. We've got to find her."

Max was struggling to stay composed. His voice was just as ragged when he assured Courtney, "We're going to bring her home, Court. Where's Jim?"

"Inside. He's calling his parents. Mom and Dad are already on their way," she answered.

Just then, I saw a man step outside the house with his head down and the phone to his ear. He started pacing back and forth as he spoke. I realized then that that was Jim.

"Okay. We just need to talk to the police and see what the first step is," Max said. I could tell he was doing everything he could to keep himself in control of his emotions. I didn't know if it was for the sake of his sister, himself, or both.

"She just wanted to play in the snow," Courtney cried softly. "We came out here so she could play."

I vaguely heard a phone ringing, but I couldn't pay attention to that because the moment the words came out of Courtney's mouth, I saw defeat and devastation come over Max's face. It hadn't snowed since the big storm, but there was still more than enough snow on the ground for a little girl to play in. Max hadn't made it over to play in the snow with Claire like he had promised. That's the moment I knew Max was never going to forgive himself for this. It was also the moment I believed he realized he'd not come to see Claire because he'd been spending that time with me.

"One minute she was right there, the next she was gone," Courtney began. "I took my eyes off of her for one second when I turned around for Julian. By the time I turned back around, the tires were squealing, and Claire's pink snowsuit being pulled into the car was the only thing I saw."

She saw the car. That had to be a good thing. That was at least *something*.

Just then, the phone in Courtney's hand rang. She looked down at it, and I watched as her brows pulled together. She slid her finger across the screen and held it to her ear. "Hello?" she answered.

Max and I watched his sister as she waited for whoever was on the other end of the line to respond. It took a matter of seconds for Courtney's face to pale and her entire body to lock. Her eyes were filled with fear as she looked up at her brother. Max must have figured out what was happening because he yelled out to his brother-in-law, "Jim!"

I looked to see Jim moving in our direction. His face was a mix of determination and anguish. A few officers who were there must have noticed something because they started following behind Jim. Before he made it over to us, my attention was turned back to Max because he'd pulled the phone from Courtney's hand.

He held it to his ear and declared, "You've got Claire's uncle, Max King."

There was silence while he listened to the person on the other end of the line. Max's eyes slid to Jim's.

"How much?" he asked a moment later.

Oh God.

Oh no.

This was bad.

"When?" he pressed, his voice tight and strained.

There was a beat of silence before Max growled, "I need more time than that."

He waited and listened.

"I want to talk to her. I need to hear her voice. I need proof she's unharmed right now."

A few seconds passed before I saw the tears well in Max's eyes. "Hi, kiddo," he struggled to get out. Max continued to break my heart when he promised, "That's right. Uncle Max is coming to get you so we can go play in the snow." Another pause, then, "Yep, we're playing hide-and-seek right now, and you've got such a good hiding spot. But I'm going to find you. I'm going to be there as soon as I can, Claire. I promise you. Okay?" He waited for her reply. And finally, he vowed, "Love you more than the world, Claire-bear."

My heart couldn't handle it. A sob crawled up the back of my throat and escaped. Max's eyes came to me, but I knew he was no longer listening to Claire. Because his entire demeanor changed.

"We will get it. You will have it. But you need to give us more time. No games. You'll get the money. But if that little girl comes back here with so much as a hair out of place, I can promise you'll wish you were dead. Because I will make it my life's mission to find you. And when I do, I'll show you no mercy."

I didn't think it was wise for Max to be threatening the guy who had his niece. I especially didn't think it was smart that he was doing that in front of the group of police officers that had moved toward us. Even still, I stayed silent. I was here to support him, not call him out on the things I didn't think were wise.

Max pulled the phone from his ear and whispered, "Fuck."

"Max?" Courtney called.

"Fuck, fuck, fuck!!" he repeated, his voice getting louder with each word.

At that point, one of the officers took charge and said, "Mr. King, please calm down. We need to know what they said so we can figure out our next move."

Max's dead eyes went to his brother-in-law before they went to the officer, and he deadpanned, "Claire was a target."

"What do you mean?" the officer asked.

Max took in a deep breath. "These guys are connected to the cartel that Jim and his team just seized that twenty-five-million-dollar shipment for. Now, they're demanding fifty million dollars in the next twelve hours if we want Claire back unharmed."

I gasped.

Ransom.

Someone took Max's innocent four-year-old niece for a fifty-million-dollar ransom.

"Oh God, Jim," Courtney cried as she fell into her husband's chest. "Our baby."

Jim took the weight of his wife's body against his, curling an arm around her, and promised, "They aren't going to get away with this. We're going to bring her home."

Max stood there staring at the ground for several

long moments before something came over him. It was like he'd had a revelation of sorts, and I knew that was true when he finally declared, "I'm going to liquidate the business. I just can't get it done as fast as they want it."

Max was going to give up his livelihood to get his niece back. My heart couldn't take it. I needed to do something. Unfortunately, before I had a chance to say anything, the officer did.

"Mr. King—" the officer got out before he was cut off.

"Max," Max insisted.

The officer jerked his chin down in acknowledgment and began again. "Max, I'm going to highly suggest you reconsider. Jim's already been in touch with some of the men he works with and we're going to call in the Feds and—" That's all he got out before Max cut it off again.

"I'm going to do whatever I need to do to bring that little girl home," he seethed. "So you can call whoever you've got to call, but don't you try to talk me out of doing what I've got to do to make sure she's safe and is home on time to sleep in her bed tonight."

Max was going to lose it. I could tell he was barely hanging on by a thread.

"We want to get her back safely, too," the officer assured him. "Did they say anything else on the call?"

"They're calling back in four hours to confirm the details of how and where they want the money sent, and to make sure we're on track for timing," Max shared.

"What about my little girl?" Jim pleaded with Max

for any shred of a connection to his daughter. "What did she say?"

"She's got to be so scared," Courtney worried, her hands clutching her husband.

Max dropped his gaze to the ground and closed his eyes. He took a few deep breaths before looking back at his sister and his brother-in-law. "Her head is still in the clouds. She's not scared, which makes me believe that whoever has her is at least being decent with her. Based on what she said, they told her we were playing hide-and-seek. I figured it was best to let her think she's winning right now."

Nobody said anything for several long moments, but Max started letting the guilt take over. "I should have taken her outside and played with her the day she asked," he mumbled.

That's when I moved to him. I slid my arms around his waist and pressed my cheek to his chest. Max's grip around me was so tight, I was being crushed to his body. He was hurting and needing my support right now, so I didn't say anything. I just let him hold on as tight as he needed.

Just then, an SUV flew up the road and came to an abrupt halt. An older man and woman jumped out and came running over in tears.

They had to be Max's parents.

Claire's grandparents.

Between their son and daughter, they were given an update on the situation. Max's mother moved to her daughter and engulfed her in her arms. Max's father looked between his son and son-in-law and asked, "What are we going to do?"

Max shook his head. "I don't have that kind of cash liquid right now. I told them I'd get them what they want, but that we needed time. They aren't budging."

"Maybe we can give them a partial payment in the time frame and then negotiate a time for the remainder," his father suggested.

"I'll try anything," Max offered. "But I need to make some calls first so I can see how much I can come up with that quick."

Max's father added, "Same here. We just need to put everything we've got together and hope they'll accept it."

"Gentlemen," an officer interrupted. When he had their attention, he explained, "I don't want to dash your hopes or anything, but in cases like this, it's very rare that they'll negotiate, especially if you've already promised them the payday they're looking for. I am strongly suggesting you wait until the FBI is here and can get a professional on the line. I'm not saying you can't try, but I want you to be prepared for what could happen if you do this. You don't want to risk insulting or angering them. That won't be good for Claire."

I stood there staring at the hopeless faces. The man I loved and his family. A family I believed I could love, too.

They were all completely, totally shattered.

This whole family was broken.

Courtney and her mother were crying in one another's arms. I could easily see Jim struggling. There wasn't a doubt in my mind that he was feeling a tremendous amount of guilt that the work he did put his little girl in harm's way. Max's father was staring off into the distance, and I wondered if he was picturing that little girl's face.

Then, there was Max.

He was...I didn't even know what he was. The look on his face wasn't something I'd ever seen before now. In fact, it was something I knew I never wanted to see again.

I had to do something.

I couldn't stand by and do nothing when I had the ability to take care of Max for a change.

So, I blurted, "When they call back in four hours and give you the details for payment, give them to me. I can have the money ready to go wherever it needs to go within an hour. Probably less."

In an instant, I could feel everyone's eyes on me, but I was only looking at Max. "What?" he asked as his head jerked back.

"Give me the account details of where they want the money sent, and I'll transfer the money to get Claire back," I semi-repeated.

"Ella...you...do you...can you—"

I cut him off and assured him, "I can."

His eyes widened. "How?" he asked.

Now was as good a time as any. I took in a deep breath, slowly let it out, and explained, "Because my name is Eleanor Page and I'm the developer, founder, owner, and every other head-honcho title you can give me of Page TV and a smattering of other widely-used apps. I literally have billions of dollars, Max. I will pay to get your niece home safe and sound and without a hair on her head out of place."

Max was utterly shocked. He clearly never expected I was this well off, and he didn't move a single muscle for a long time.

"We can't ask you to do that, Ella," he insisted after several minutes had passed.

"You didn't," I told him. "I'm offering."

Max continued to stare at me. I held his eyes.

When I spoke again, I stated, "It's time to tip the scales in my favor."

CHAPTER 10

Eleanor

THE CHARGE OF ELECTRICITY AND TENSION IN THE AIR WAS palpable. I'd finally found the way to tell Max the truth about who I was, and he had yet to really react. Suddenly, I was wondering if I should have stepped in.

I mean, a little girl was missing. A little girl Max loved. Doing nothing just wasn't an option for me.

But Max's inability to speak to me was starting to worry me.

In fact, when I told him it was time to tip the scales, all he did was close his eyes and let out a sigh.

"Max?" Courtney called, breaking the silence.

Max turned to his sister who had her eyes on me. Understanding the question in her tone, Max introduced us. "Court, this is Ella. Ella, this is Courtney."

I stepped forward and extended my hand to her. "Hi, Courtney. It's so nice to finally meet you. I wish we were meeting under better circumstances, oof—"

Courtney hadn't taken my hand to shake. Instead, she used it to yank me toward her where she pulled me into a hug and held on tight. She didn't say anything. She just held me fiercely. And that was all I needed to know not only just how much this meant to her, but also that I'd done the right thing. At least, it was the right thing in her mind. I still had no clue what Max's thoughts were.

From that point forward, I didn't remember or pay much attention to what was happening around me. The police were there, the Feds were on their way, and a handful of members of Max's extended family had arrived. But I found it incredibly difficult to focus on any of it.

Because all of my attention was on Max. Initially, it was on the fact that he seemed to be in such a state of shock. But then it was because he moved from that to conflicted. I already felt so horrible for everyone involved in the situation that I didn't want to make assumptions about Max's headspace. So, I stood by and waited for any indication of what I could do.

The only time I pulled myself away from Max's side was when his nephew, Julian, started getting fussy. I knew I was an unfamiliar face, but the whole family was so torn up over Claire being kidnapped for ransom that I had a feeling Julian could sense it. I walked over and bent down where he was seated on the floor. There were a bunch of toys out for him to play with; however, with everyone else being so distraught, Julian didn't have anybody to play with him.

So, while Max and his family talked to the police and the FBI after they arrived, answered their questions, and cried, I occupied Julian. But I didn't do it without looking over at Max regularly to make sure he was okay. It hurt my heart to see, more often than not, that he wasn't. Because if he wasn't on the phone or speaking with detectives with determination written all over his face, he was staring off into space looking defeated.

Three and a half hours after they received the first call, the phone rang again. It was from a blocked number, so we knew it was them. And even though the FBI had arrived and walked Max through what he needed to do and say, everyone seemed to be feeling a little anxious. This was mostly because the kidnappers were calling thirty minutes sooner than they originally said they would.

When Max answered the phone, it was like nobody in the room was even breathing.

"You've got Max," he answered.

Despite the number of people in the room, my eyes remained focused on Max. Based on what I gathered from the earlier conversations, I knew there was an FBI agent listening in to the call. But I didn't seek out that person at that moment.

I only cared about Max.

I watched from where I was sitting on the floor playing with Julian, as Max's body grew more and more rigid. He was holding a pen in one of his hands, looking down at the notepad, and scribbling what I could only assume were the account details for the transfer.

"Where?" Max asked.

He listened and waited for a response.

Max's eyes shot to the agent I assumed was listening in. The agent nodded and held up two fingers.

"Two hours," Max stated.

He listened again, and suddenly, his face got angry.

"We do it in two hours, and she's home with her family tonight," he growled.

The federal agent got close, got Max's attention, and somehow silently communicated that Max needed to pull it together.

Not even a minute later, the call was disconnected.

Jim didn't wait. "What did they say?" he asked.

After getting a nod from the agent, Max looked at his sister, his brother-in-law, and finally me before he declared, "They want the money transferred via Page Pay."

Wow. One of my other apps was going to be used to facilitate the collection of a ransom. This was awful.

"What?" Jim asked, evidently confused.

Max stood and looked at me. "I assume that's yours as well?" he asked.

I offered a quick dip of my chin in return, but at the same time, I wondered what was going through his mind. Was he relieved it was my app or was he annoyed that I'd created something that made me a lot of money, and now that app was going to be involved in transferring funds to ensure the safe return of his niece?

Before Max could say anything else, Courtney pleaded, "We're going to get her back today, right? She's going to be home tonight?"

At that point, the federal agent who'd been listening in to the call took a step forward and explained, "They don't want to release Claire until the funds have cleared. Normally, a transaction through an app like that is immediate; however, sometimes there can be holds put on it. Given the size of the ransom that Max already agreed to give them, it's likely there will be a hold on the funds. It can take up to seventy-two hours sometimes to have the funds released."

"They can't keep her," Courtney cried.

I decided to step in. "I can take care of the hold," I started. "It's my app and my software. I'll see to it that the funds are released immediately, but I will not make that transfer until we see that Claire is safe."

"Ma'am?" the agent directed his attention to me.

I stood from my spot on the floor next to Julian and extended my hand to him. "Eleanor Page, sir."

He took my hand, shook it, and returned, "Agent Palmer. You said this is your app?"

I nodded. "Yes, I'm an app developer and Page Pay is one of mine. I handle all of the development and tech for it, and I'll easily be able to lift the hold on the funds."

Agent Palmer looked at me curiously for a moment before he asked, "Do you have a means for tracking the recipient, Ms. Page?"

I smiled and confirmed, "Yes. And please, call me Eleanor."

"Okay, I'm going to have you sit down and talk with one of the other agents about the technical side of that if you don't mind," he remarked.

"Absolutely. Anything I can do to help get Claire back here safely and see to it that these people can't ever do this again," I assured him.

Agent Palmer looked at Courtney, Jim, and Max, and

advised, "Give me a minute. I'm going to get Eleanor set up with one of the other agents. After I do that, we'll discuss what the plan is for when they call back."

At that, Agent Palmer led me out of the room to meet with Agent Garza. When he left to get back to Max, Courtney, Jim, and the rest of their family, I sat down with Agent Garza and explained everything he needed to know about how my app worked, what data it collected, and how he could use it to locate the kidnappers.

He even drove me back to my house, so that I could get my laptop. Even though I didn't typically work on my laptop, mostly because I liked having a large screen to look at when I was working, the laptop still had all the programs necessary to do what had to be done today.

Just under two hours later, the phone rang again. Max was instructed to put the phone on speaker so that I'd be able to listen in and confirm if anything the kidnappers were saying wouldn't be possible.

"Max King," he answered.

"Down the road from the post office on Chickadee Avenue, there's a park. It's got a big hill where kids go sledding. Your niece is on her way there right now. You've got fifteen minutes to get there. There's a sniper on her, so do not approach her until you hear from me. I'll call with the payment address. Once I've got it and it's been transferred out of the account, we'll call off the sniper and you'll be free to get her."

The line went dead.

There was silence for about half a second before Agent Palmer ordered, "Max and Eleanor, you're both going with me. Mr. and Mrs. Golden, since you need Claire's car seat, Agent Booker will ride along with you."

As we began moving toward the door, Agent Palmer shouted orders to his team and the local police department. The most important of those was that aside from him pulling up close in the unmarked vehicle with me and Max, and Agent Booker riding with Claire's parents, the rest were to remain at a distance until Claire was safe.

"Stay with Julian!" Courtney yelled out to her parents.

"Bring our girl home safe," her father demanded.

That was the last thing I heard before we raced out the door.

Twelve minutes had passed between the time the call with the kidnappers ended and the time we arrived at the park. Looking out the window, it suddenly became clear to me why they chose this park. With all the snow we'd received two weeks ago, there were a lot of kids and quite a few adults there as well.

There were kids at the top of the hill, kids at the bottom, and a bunch of them in the midst of riding a sled down the hill. My eyes scanned through everyone looking for a little girl that could be Claire. I believed I'd finally found her and declared, "That's got to be her."

"You see her?" Agent Palmer asked.

"She's the little girl in the bright pink snowsuit at the bottom of the hill trying to climb back up to the top," Max confirmed.

His hand went to the door handle, but Agent Palmer stopped him. "Patience, Max. I know it's hard, but be patient. I've got a team searching the surrounding areas for anywhere a sniper could be sitting. There's another one checking for any vehicles in the area that match the description of the one your sister gave to the detectives. They had to get her here somehow."

Poor Claire.

Poor Max.

I felt horrible for the entire family.

All I wanted to do was get out of the car and run over to the little girl. Luckily, we didn't have to exercise too much patience because Courtney's phone, which Max still had, rang in his hand.

"We're here," Max answered.

"I didn't doubt it," the kidnapper replied. "Are you ready to make the payment?"

Max and Agent Palmer's eyes came to me. I already had my laptop out and had set up a hotspot, so I gave them a nod.

"Yes, we're ready," Max replied.

The kidnapper rattled off the email address associated with the account the money was to be sent to. I entered it in and continued the process of sending a payment by filling in the rest of the required details. Once I had everything all set to send the payment, I looked up and mouthed, "Send?"

Agent Palmer gave me a nod.

I sent the payment, saw there was a hold put on it, and immediately worked on the back end to release the funds into the payee's account. After I'd done that, I brought my eyes to Max and whispered, "It's done."

"The money's been sent," Max declared.

There was a beat of silence before he received a response. "Yes, I can see it just arrived. You'll wait until I've transferred it out."

We had no choice. If there was a chance they had a sniper on Claire, we couldn't take that risk. So, we waited. And I watched as Max's eyes never left Claire.

Finally, after what felt like hours, we heard, "I've transferred the funds out of the account and called off my sniper. It's been a pleasure doing business with you, Mr. King. You're free to get your niece."

Max didn't even wait to disconnect. He dropped the phone and was out the door. I got out behind him, but he was already taking off. Glancing behind Agent Palmer's car, I saw Jim and Courtney exiting their vehicle. We took one look at each other and they were off.

I started moving in that direction, but I didn't run. I hadn't ever met Claire and didn't want her overwhelmed.

"Claire!" Max yelled as he ran toward her. It didn't seem he cared that most of the adults standing around had turned to look at him.

When Claire spun around at the sound of her name being called and saw her uncle running in her direction, she threw her hands up in the air and called out excitedly, "Uncle Max!"

The little girl moved as fast as her little legs would allow in her big, puffy snowsuit until finally she collided with Max. He picked her up, pulled her tight to his chest, and kissed her cheeks.

"You found me," she squealed.

"Of course, Claire. I wouldn't have ever stopped looking for you," he promised her.

Courtney and Jim made it to Max and Claire.

"Mommy! Daddy! Everybody came to play!"

"Oh, baby," Courtney cried, taking Claire from Max's arms.

"Are you okay, sweet pea?" Jim asked his daughter after he'd put one arm around her and the other around his wife.

While they poured their affections over their daughter, I looked at Max. His eyes were filled with unshed tears as he looked at the little girl who seemed to have no clue of the ordeal her family had just been through.

Max eventually turned his eyes to me, but he never had a chance to say anything because Agents Palmer and Booker had come up beside us.

"Folks, why don't we make our way back to the cars so we can get her home?" Agent Palmer suggested.

With that, we all turned and moved back to the cars.

It was several hours later when Max and I were back in his truck on the way home. He was quiet, as he'd been with me most of the day. Part of me wanted to talk to him and make sure he was doing okay, but the other part of me felt it was wise to let him be the one to lead the discussion.

It had been a long emotional day for everyone. After

Claire was rescued, we'd all gone back to her family's home. While there weren't as many officers in her house as there had been before she was rescued, there were still a handful hanging around tying up some loose ends with the family. She didn't seem the least bit bothered by having all the extra people around.

At one point, a few minutes before Max and I left, Claire asked, "Who's that?"

"Who?" Courtney wondered.

Claire pointed at me and stated, "Her. The lady next to Uncle Max."

Courtney stood, with Claire in her arms, and moved toward us. "This is Uncle Max's girlfriend, Eleanor."

I'd just been officially introduced to Max's niece as his girlfriend. Of course, I knew that's what Courtney assumed I was. Heck, it was what I assumed I was. But with the way Max had been acting since he'd learned the truth about me, I wasn't sure things would remain that way. And it saddened me to think this little girl was being introduced to me in such a way when it might not last beyond the night. I tried to push the negative thoughts away and brought myself back to the people standing in front of me.

I offered Claire a bright smile and said, "It's so nice to meet you, Claire."

"You're pretty," she marveled.

I let out a laugh. "That's so sweet of you to say. I think you are one beautiful girl, too."

"Can you play in the snow with me and Uncle Max?"

"Well, your Uncle Max and I are getting ready to

leave now," I explained. I wasn't sure if I was overstepping when I suggested it, but I added, "But maybe I can come and join you another time. Besides, I totally didn't bring my snowsuit with me this time."

Her eyes widened. "Mommy says I can't go out in the snow without my snowsuit and hat and gloves on."

"That's right. You have to make sure you stay warm," I agreed.

Max reached out and took Claire from her mom. "Give me hugs and kisses, Claire-bear. I've got to get going now."

Claire wrapped her tiny arms around Max's neck and squeezed him tight. Then, she gave him kisses before he handed her back over to her mom. Courtney seemed to be having a tough time with letting go of Claire. I figured that would fade as the time ticked by.

Max and I said goodbye and left.

And now, we'd made it back to our neighborhood in complete silence. When Max stopped at the top of my driveway, he turned off the truck and came around to meet me on my side. I opened my front door and stepped inside, but Max didn't follow me in.

"Max?" I called, turning back to look at him standing on the other side of the door frame.

His troubled eyes came to mine. "I'm going to call it a night here, Ella. I think I just need to go home and be by myself for a while."

Oh God.

Oh no.

"Are you sure?" I asked.

Nodding, he answered, "Yeah."

I got it. Or, at least, I hoped I did. This had to have been the most grueling day of his entire life. I couldn't begin to imagine the thoughts running through his mind. But I truly didn't think he'd want to be alone with those thoughts. I believed he'd want someone to unload them on. It worried me that he wouldn't want to unload them on me, especially when I knew that he'd learned something so shocking about me only hours ago.

"Don't you think it might help to talk about what you're feeling right now?" I asked.

"Maybe," he answered with a shrug. "But considering I'm not quite sure I even know what I'm feeling right now, I don't know how I could do that. I really just need to be alone right now."

This was it.

I knew where things were heading.

And because Max meant as much as he did to me, I had to step in and do something about it. He had been through a lot today; it couldn't have been easy for him. So, I decided I needed to make the effort for the both of us right now.

My eyes were pleading with his when I begged, "Please come in, Max. We don't have to talk about it right now, but I'd rather know I'm right by your side if you change your mind."

I did my best to swallow past the lump forming in my throat as I waited for him to respond.

Max hesitated. I could see him struggling with what he wanted to do.

"Okay," Max agreed as he gave a slight downward jerk of his chin and stepped inside.

Relief swept through me even though I knew there was still so much unresolved between us. Max locked the door behind him.

"Can I make you something to eat?" I asked, thinking that food always helped in situations like this.

Max shook his head. "I'm good," he insisted. "But if you're hungry, you should eat."

I didn't want to eat. My stomach was already churning at the unknown. I had only offered him food because I was simply planning to use food as a way to break the tension.

"I'm good," I repeated his words.

Max dipped his chin and muttered, "It's been a long day. We should probably get some sleep."

I nervously bit my lip before I gave him a nod. "Yeah. Okay," I agreed.

At that, I turned off the lights on the first floor before climbing the stairs with Max following behind me. When we made it to the bedroom, I asked, "Did you want to use the shower first?"

"You go," he insisted.

"You could join me," I offered. I didn't know if that was the right thing to do in a situation like this, but I was willing to try anything. I'd managed to get him to stay, but I didn't think my efforts should have just stopped there. I was prepared to do whatever it took to either distract him from whatever horrible thoughts were still lingering in his mind about what happened to Claire or convince him to open up and share his worries with me.

Sadly, Max declined my invitation. "Not tonight," he said.

Feeling disappointed but trying not to let it show, I turned and walked away from him. While I went into the bathroom, he stayed in my bedroom. And as I stood under the hot spray of the shower, I began to wonder what I should do.

I was feeling a lot of regret about how I shared the truth of who I was with Max. Never did I imagine a situation like this would occur where I'd end up having no choice but to blurt everything out the way that I did. But it happened, and there wasn't anything I could do to change it. All I knew now was that I was terrified that Max's change in demeanor meant that we were at the beginning of the end of us.

Sadness consumed me at the thought.

And I hated the way that felt.

As I finished up in the shower, I realized I had a choice to make. Either I could sit around wondering where Max's head was, or I could come out and ask him. The distance he was currently putting between us was precisely the thing I'd been worried about from the beginning. And I knew that if I didn't step in and say something now, things were just going to get worse.

With my mind made up, I got out of the shower and toweled off.

When I entered my bedroom again, I found Max on his back in the bed with the fingers of one hand rubbing his eyes. He never stopped to look over at me. If ever there was a time when Max didn't join me in the shower, he was always guaranteed to watch me when I walked out.

It seemed he wouldn't be doing that tonight.

I got myself dressed and climbed in the bed beside him. Feeling nervous about his mood, I figured it was best to stick to my side of the bed.

I waited a few minutes, but Max made no attempt to say anything to me. So, I knew I was going to have to be the one to do it.

"Max?" I called quietly.

"Yeah?" he replied, his eyes never looking in my direction.

"Is everything…are we okay?" I asked.

His hand stopped moving over his eyes, but he still never looked my way. "What do you mean?" he wondered.

Did he really not know what I meant?

"Well, it's just that you've been a bit distant the last few hours," I started. "I know a lot happened today, but I think we need to talk about this."

His head snapped in my direction. On one hand I was grateful to finally have his eyes on me, but on the other, he wasn't giving me an adoring look.

"Now?" he asked incredulously. "You think we should talk about this now?"

My eyes darted back and forth. I thought now was as good a time as any. In fact, I thought it was best to talk about it now when it was still fresh in our minds. He could get out whatever he was feeling, and I'd hopefully feel some relief that he wasn't completely put off by my success.

"Um, yeah. I was kind of hoping you could tell me what's going through your mind," I explained.

"I already told you that it's been a long day," he began. "Right now, I've got entirely too much going through my mind. I'm really not up for talking about it all right now."

"We don't have to talk about all of it," I assured him. "I just want to know—"

"Look," he cut me off as he sat up in the bed. "I don't want to talk about *any* of it right now. Hell, I don't even want to think about any of it right now. But I am. Because all I keep thinking about is the fact that my niece was kidnapped today. Claire was kidnapped and I found out my woman lied to me."

I gasped.

Fuck.

My throat was tight when I rasped, "I didn't lie to you, Max."

"You hid something from me that was pretty fucking important," he shot back.

"I never meant to—"

Max cut me off again. "I need some time to process all of this. I'm not trying to be an ungrateful prick because I really do appreciate how you stepped up today for Claire. Thank you. I hope you know I genuinely mean that. But at the same time, I've got a lot messing with my head that I'm trying to come to terms with right now."

"Max, I…" I trailed off. I didn't know if I'd found the right words, and I definitely didn't know if this was the right time to share them, but after what happened today and what I believed was happening between us now, I didn't like the idea of waiting. So, I clarified, "I did what I did for Claire today, but really, I did it for you. I love you, Max. And if I had to do it again for you, I wouldn't hesitate."

Something I couldn't read washed over him. The look terrified me. But what he did next scared me more. Without any acknowledgment of those three little words I'd just shared, Max stood and walked to the bathroom. He was in there for quite a long time. And when he came back, he simply got in the bed next to me and said, "Try to get some sleep."

There was no way that was going to happen with all of this unresolved business between us.

But Max was clearly done talking.

Just before he reached over to the nightstand to turn out the light, he held my eyes briefly, shook his head, and whispered, "Goodnight."

I didn't respond.

Seconds after he turned out the light, he added, "Eleanor Page."

After that, I didn't think I'd ever manage to find sleep. But somehow, I must have. Because when I woke early the next morning, well before the sun rose, Max was gone and there was a note on his pillow.

Couldn't sleep. Needed some time alone to think, so I went home. -Max

Once I read that, I knew.

Max was done with me. It was only a matter of time before he completely distanced himself from me and broke my heart for good.

CHAPTER 11

Eleanor

"**G**OOD MORNING, MAX. IT'S ME, ELLA. YOU PROBABLY already know that from my number, though. Anyway, I just wanted to check in and make sure you're doing alright. Give me a call when you can."

It had been fourteen hours and thirty-six minutes since Max called me Eleanor Page and pretended to fall asleep beside me. No kiss goodnight. No peck on the cheek. No darling. Nothing. Just a thank you, goodnight, a shake of his head, and my full name. And, of course, a note.

I tried holding out this morning, hoping he'd call or stop by. But eventually I couldn't stand it any longer and gave into my urge to check on him. I was worried about him, and I was worried about us. So, I called him and got his voicemail. It concerned me, but I tried to give him the benefit of the doubt. I told myself that he was probably exercising or taking a shower. I figured if I didn't hear from him by lunchtime, I'd try again.

For the next three hours, I kept myself busy around the house. Even though there really wasn't a mess in my home, I started the task of reorganizing. I started in my kitchen. I went through and got rid of items I purchased back when I moved in that hadn't been used and already expired. I cleaned out the entire refrigerator. I reorganized my drawers and cabinets. I even mopped the floor that had just been mopped two days ago.

Just after lunchtime, when I could no longer stop myself, I called Max again.

"You've got Max. Leave me a message."

I took in a deep breath and said, "It's me again. I hope you're okay. Please call me. I just want to know that you're alright."

Disappointed, I disconnected and walked upstairs to my bedroom. It was time to reorganize my closet. I pulled every item I hadn't worn in the last year and evaluated it. Ninety percent of those items were boxed up and set aside. I'd do some research and find a local woman's shelter where I could donate them. The remaining ten percent were pieces that I truly loved. I was going to give myself another year to have a place to wear them. If I didn't, I'd reevaluate. Once I'd finished with the clothes, I moved on to my shoes. My entire closet project took me hours. In fact, I hadn't completely finished when dinnertime rolled around. I wasn't hungry, but I needed a change of scenery. Leaving my unfinished closet, I decided I couldn't wait around for Max's call.

I grabbed my keys, locked up, and went to Max's place. For five long agonizing minutes, I stood outside his house in the bitter cold. I rang the bell. I knocked on the door. He never answered.

Feeling downtrodden, I went back home. Then, I tackled my office. My home was generally spotless, so there wasn't much of a mess to pick up. It was merely reorganization and purging. Two hours later, I gave into the feelings I tried to avoid feeling all day and plopped myself down in my big, comfortable office chair. I sat, staring out the window, at Max's house.

Why was he avoiding me? I asked myself the question but was afraid I already knew the answer.

Ten minutes after I sat down, I watched as Max drove his truck up his driveway. His garage door went up, and he pulled in. I felt the slightest bit of relief that he hadn't been in the house simply ignoring me when I went over there to check on him.

A second vehicle came up the driveway, pulling up right behind where Max had parked. I saw him standing at the back of his truck, waiting.

Then, my stomach twisted in knots as I watched a woman in a tight skirt and heels get out of the car. Max waited for her to round the front of her car toward him. He slid an arm around her and gave her a hug before allowing her to walk ahead of him into the house.

Minutes later, the light in his bedroom went on.

I sat in my chair, tears rolling down my cheeks, for the next hour and a half, which was when the woman finally left.

I should have listened. My mom and my friends both urged me to tell him right upfront. I didn't. I was so stupid.

Stupid.

Stupid.

Stupid.

For allowing myself to get involved this deep with a man before I shared who I was with him. Before I knew whether his pride would allow him to be with someone who might have made more money than him but would love him the same even if she weren't successful.

After the woman drove off, I continued to sit in my office as tears rolled down my cheeks. I did that for the next twenty minutes. Finally, when Max's bedroom light went off without him bothering to return my calls, I took myself upstairs, climbed in my bed, and cried myself to sleep.

"You were right," I admitted into the phone, the anguish in my voice unable to be disguised.

It was the morning after Max had officially broken my heart and crushed it to pieces. I was on the phone with Maggie.

"What? Ella, what's wrong?" she asked.

"I fell in love with him, Mags. I fell in love with a man who didn't know who I was. And once he found out, he scraped me off."

I just barely heard her swear under her breath. "What happened?" she pressed for more information.

There was no time like the present. I launched in and told Maggie what happened. I gave her everything that I'd shared with Steph only a few days earlier, but I also added the whole situation with Claire. I did not tell her about the woman from last night. It was hard enough to admit to myself. Sharing it with someone else would have been an impossible task.

When I finished telling my friend all the awful details of the horrible situation I'd put myself in, she lamented, "Oh, babe. I'm so sorry. Do you think maybe he just needs some time to process everything? I mean, his niece was kidnapped for ransom. And it sounds like if you hadn't been willing or able to step up to the plate for them, that little girl might not have made it home. Surely, that's got to be weighing heavily on his mind."

That made sense, and I completely understood where she was coming from. That didn't negate the fact that not only did he not even have the decency to return one of my calls yesterday, but he also had a woman at his house not even twenty-four hours after he'd left mine. If this was about Claire and needing time to cope with what happened, I would have thought he'd at least call. A text message would have sufficed. Or, at least, it would have until I saw what I saw last night.

I didn't share any of this with Maggie. Instead, I lied, "Yeah, I guess that's possible."

"It wasn't just that, though, Ella," she went on.

"What do you mean?"

"Well, think about it," she began. "Not only does all of this happen to the little girl that you said he adores, but amidst everything going on with that, he learns that the woman he's with is a billionaire. There were guys who weren't dealing with everything Max was, and they couldn't handle it. Maybe it was too much all at once and he just needs a little time."

"Or maybe he's just like the rest of them," I suggested.

There was a moment of hesitation before she advised, "If that were true, you wouldn't be this heartbroken."

I wanted to believe that. Max had seemed so different than any other man. I truly never believed he would have just written me off like he did. And because Maggie didn't know about the woman who spent an hour and a half in Max's bedroom last night, she was doing her best to be supportive of me and give Max the benefit of the doubt. At least, of course, until I had confirmation from Max that it was over between us. Then, and only then, would she and Steph both be there to dry my tears and tell me how I was better off without him.

That's what bothered me the most about all of it, though. Max didn't even give me the courtesy of a proper breakup. Sure, we hadn't been together all that long, but there had been something between us. Something that, at least for me, had been special. Didn't I deserve to have the man who was sleeping with me to at least tell me that it wasn't going to work out between us?

"I don't know, Mags. I guess I've got to just pick myself up and move on."

"Don't give up hope, Ella," she pleaded. "Even if it's not Max, your guy is out there somewhere. I promise."

Not wanting to worry her more than I already knew she was, I assured her, "I won't."

Maggie and I talked for a little bit longer before we disconnected. Then, I spent the rest of my morning and early afternoon curled up on the couch watching sappy movies and crying. It certainly felt like I was a glutton for punishment.

It was around two o'clock that afternoon when there was a knock at my door. I peeled myself off the couch and went to it. Pulling it open, I found Max standing on the other side. He didn't seem to be nearly as torn up over us. The minute he saw my face, which I was certain had to be red, blotchy, and puffy-eyed, he stated, "You've been crying."

"Movies," I mumbled, offering him an explanation I wasn't convinced he deserved.

He shook his head in disbelief. "It's more than that," he asserted.

Of course it was, but that didn't mean I was prepared to tell him about it. "That's not really your concern anymore, though, is it?"

Max's chin jerked back. "Excuse me? What's with the attitude?"

"Is there something I can help you with?" I asked, trying to come across as irritated as possible.

He managed to get past my foul mood and explained, "Well, I was stopping over to let you know that I just got a call from Courtney about five minutes ago. She and Jim were on their way over with the kids, and they wanted to see you. My sister, in particular. But I'm thinking that maybe now isn't a good time."

Damn. I liked Courtney. And Jim. Of course, I'd done some bonding with Julian, and Claire was the absolute cutest.

"No, it's fine. Great, actually," I returned. "You can send them over when they arrive. I'd be happy to see them and was curious how they were all doing since everything happened. Of course, I didn't have any way to contact them myself, and I didn't want to just show up on their doorstep."

There was no lack of attitude in my response to Max. And he didn't miss it. Unfortunately for him, he took too long to reply, so I asked, "Is there something else you needed other than to inform me of the impending visit from your family?"

"You're pissed at me," he stated the obvious.

I let out a laugh. "I wish. I wish so much that I *could* be pissed at you right now. Because we both know that I should be," I responded, my voice getting quieter with each word that passed my lips.

Before Max had the chance to respond, we saw his sister's family pull into the driveway in their SUV. Max's eyes came back to mine. "We have to talk," he insisted.

I shook my head. No way. I had nothing to say. "There's nothing to talk about. You wrote me off and replaced me like that," I accused him with a snap of my fingers.

He had the audacity to appear confused. I watched as that look washed over him, but before he could say anything, Claire came running down the walkway shouting for her uncle.

"Uncle Max!" she cried out in excitement carrying a piece of paper in her hand.

Seeing that little girl running, happy, and blissfully unaware of what had happened to her not even a full two days ago helped to brighten my mood. It felt good knowing that I was able to do something to help save her from what could have been an impossibly horrific situation.

Max quickly shook off whatever was on his mind and squatted to catch Claire in his arms. The second she collided with him, he gave her a kiss on the cheek and returned, "Hey, Claire-bear."

"Look what I did!" she squealed holding up her paper. "I made a picture. It has the whole family on it. There's Mommy and Daddy. That's me. I drew a purple dress on me because it's my favorite color. That's Julian. His eyes are closed because he always sleeps so much. That's you. And that's Auntie Nora."

I struggled and failed to stop the noise that came from the back of my throat.

My heart.

I wanted to cry.

Max's niece called me Auntie Nora. I didn't even know how she knew to call me that, but I loved hearing it. I also hated knowing that, after today, I'd never hear it again.

Max looked up at me, and I knew he saw the tears in my eyes. There was so much concern and even a little bit of regret written all over his face. Sadly, no matter how much he might have regretted sleeping with someone else before officially breaking things off with me, I knew

I was the kind of girl who wouldn't be able to ever get over that.

I looked away from Max, took in a deep breath, and somehow managed to pull myself together.

Just then, Jim and Courtney made it to the door with Julian in tow. "Hi," Courtney greeted me. "I'm so sorry for the last-minute notice. We wanted to see you yesterday, but Jim's parents arrived in town. We had hoped you would have come over with Max, but since you didn't, we figured we'd just come to you."

Well, that answered part of the question of where Max went yesterday. Of course, the visit to his family's house was probably long before he stopped and picked up a woman somewhere.

I did my best to put on a happy face and beamed, "Oh, that's alright. Come on in. It's so good to see all of you."

Everyone filed inside, and I put in an abundance of effort to keep my eyes from going to Max. As much as it hurt having him there, knowing what he'd done last night, I wasn't going to kick him out and yell at him in front of a four-year-old girl and a ten-month-old baby boy. I could be an adult.

"Let me take your coats," I urged, doing anything to keep myself occupied and focused on something other than Max.

Courtney gave me hers before Jim handed his over. Claire had taken hers off and dropped it on the floor at her feet. Max picked it up and followed me to the closet after I'd ushered everyone into the family room.

Then, I made quick work of hanging the coats. Max's presence at my back was hard to ignore, but I powered through.

Just as I closed the door, Max's fingers curled around my wrist. "Ella," he started, but I quickly pulled my arm back.

Using his surprise at my reaction to his touch in my favor, I exclaimed, "Drinks!"

With that, I spun on my heels and took off in the opposite direction toward his sister and her family. "Can I get you some drinks?" I asked when I entered the room. "I've got water, soda, orange juice, sweet tea, and wine. I even have some beer here. I don't drink it, but my father likes to have a beer or two every day. So, I have some left from when my parents were here at Christmastime."

"Sweet tea, please," Courtney replied.

"A beer is good," Jim put in.

"Perfect," I declared before jerking my head to Claire. "Is orange juice okay for her? Or just water?"

"I've got a cup of water with a lid for her, so she's good for now," Courtney confirmed.

I gave her a nod of understanding. And because I wasn't going to be rude, I turned to Max. "Anything for you?"

"I'll come with and help you," he stated.

Crap.

I did not want to be alone with him right now. Because I knew when I said what I had to say I was going to end up crying. Poor Claire did not need to witness that. I couldn't possibly bring myself to pop the happy little bubble she lived in.

"Auntie Nora?" Claire called.

My heart skipped a beat as my eyes went to hers. "Yes, honey?"

"Where should I put my picture?" she asked, looking around for what I assumed would be a safe spot.

My eyes darted back and forth before I suggested, "Well, do you want to give it to your mom or dad to hold so that you don't forget it here?"

She shook her head. "No, this is for you."

"You drew that picture for me?" I asked even though she'd already told me she did.

Claire nodded her reply.

I stood up straight, held out my hand to her, and announced, "Well, then that deserves a spot front and center on my refrigerator. How about you come with me to the kitchen while I'm getting the drinks so you can find the perfect magnet and perfect place to hang it?"

Claire bounced over to me, took my hand, and walked with me to the kitchen. When we made it there, she looked up at my refrigerator, and she marveled, "That's so many magnets."

I let out a laugh and admitted, "I know. It really is. I don't have a lot of things I collect, but I like collecting magnets for this very reason. I was hoping one day I'd be able to fill my refrigerator with beautiful pictures."

"You don't have any now," she noted the obvious as she looked at the sad refrigerator with only magnets covering it.

Nodding, I agreed, "You're right. That's why your picture is super, extra special. It's the very first one, and I'm never going to take it down."

The smile on her face got so big, it lit up the room.

"Okay, you look through these while I get everybody drinks. Then, we'll hang it up together, alright?"

Claire agreed.

So, I quickly pulled the carafe with the sweet tea out of the fridge along with a beer. As Claire perused the magnets, I got out glasses for the tea. At that point, Max had entered the kitchen.

"You can grab yourself a beer if you'd like one," I offered, keeping my eyes focused on what I was doing. "I can also get you a glass of tea if you'd prefer."

I heard Max instruct, "Take two steps back, so I can open the fridge, Claire."

Good. He was getting his own beer.

I finished pouring a glass of tea each for both Courtney and myself when Max was in my space. "Ella, what—" he got out before I cut him off.

"Don't," I ordered, my eyes spearing him. "Not now. *Please,* not now."

Max studied me, his look more than slightly bewildered.

"I found one!" Claire interrupted at the perfect moment.

My gaze went to her as I said, "Oh, let me see which one you chose." I walked around Max toward Claire. She showed me the magnet she chose before I picked her up and let her select whatever she deemed the best spot on the refrigerator to hang it. Once it was in the perfect place, I set her down on her feet again and moved back to the drinks. I picked up the two glasses of tea while Max grabbed Jim's beer.

For the next three hours, I sat on a couch opposite of Jim and Courtney. Max was seated next to me. I didn't get up and move because I really didn't want to cause a scene. But it was hard to sit there next to him. Especially when he threw his arm around me and rested it on the back of the couch.

The visit with Max's sister and her family was mostly spent talking about the kids. Claire was a great source of entertainment and distraction. Courtney had asked about my family, my life in Florida, and ultimately, my career. I shared openly. It's not like I had anything to lose anymore.

But as it approached dinnertime, Courtney finally remarked, "We should probably get going so we can get the kids back to Grandma and Grandpa's for dinner, baths, and bedtime."

That was another thing I'd learned during their visit. Part of what they'd decided was to stay temporarily with Courtney's parents until progress could be made on the case. Given that their family was specifically targeted because of Jim's line of work, they wanted to take precautionary measures for the time being. The security was a bit tighter at Courtney and Max's parents' place, so they figured it was the best spot for an immediate solution. Either way, Courtney wasn't letting Claire or Julian out of her sight.

"Well, it was so nice of you to stop by," I began as I stood. "It's a bummer you're not back in your house yet, but I'm happy you're all managing okay. If you need anything, I'll give you my number. Please don't hesitate to reach out to me."

"Claire, how about you give Auntie Nora a hug and a kiss before you go with Daddy to get your jacket on?"

Claire did as she was told and came over to give me a hug and a kiss. I held her tight for a moment before her dad urged, "Come on, sweet pea."

Courtney walked over to me, Julian resting on her hip, and reached for my hand. I was acutely aware of the fact that Max was standing right beside me. Squeezing tight, her voice just a touch over a whisper, Courtney stated, "I didn't want to do this because of Claire. She listens and hears everything, and I don't want her to know that anything was ever wrong."

Shaking my head, I tried to ease her concerns. "Courtney, I would never say a word about it to her. And you don't have to worry that because I am who I am that Claire's situation will ever become public. I can promise you that'll never happen."

"I appreciate that, but that's not my concern," she returned.

"Oh. What's wrong?" I asked.

She held my eyes for several long moments before she rasped, "How can I ever thank you for what you did for Claire?"

"There's no need," I insisted. "I have a picture hanging on my fridge right now that is really all the thanks I want."

She closed her eyes and squeezed my hand tighter. "Thank you," she whispered when she opened them.

"Don't worry about it. Really. Besides, I already kind of owed Max."

Her head tipped to the side. She eyed Max curiously before she looked back at me. "For what?" she wondered.

Of its own accord, my neck craned and I looked up at Max. I stared at his handsome face as I answered quietly, "He plowed my driveway."

I heard a laugh come from Courtney before she advised, "I hate to break it to you, Ella, but what Max did for you was nothing in comparison."

Returning my attention to her, I shook my head and somehow managed to speak past the lump in my throat when I confessed, "It was so much more, Courtney."

Realizing there was no point in trying to argue with me, she gave me a nod and let go of my hand. We walked out into the foyer where we met Jim and Claire. I gave out a round of hugs to everyone, except for Max, and moved with them to the door.

With Courtney holding Julian and Jim carrying Claire, I watched the beautiful family walk away from my house and back to their car.

Max did not follow them.

CHAPTER 12

Eleanor

WHEN I TURNED AND SAW THAT MAX WAS MAKING NO effort to leave, I recommended, "It would be best if you would leave now, too."

He followed me back into the house, closed the door, and crossed his arms over his chest. "What is going on with you?" he asked.

I raised my eyebrows in disbelief. "Me? What's going on with me?" I shot back. "I don't know, Max. What do you think could possibly be wrong with me?"

"I don't have much to go on here, but my best guess is that you're pissed I didn't return your calls yesterday," he bit out.

"Yeah, how about we start there?" I suggested. "You're right. I am pissed that you didn't return my calls yesterday. I don't understand what would have been so hard about that."

"Ella, I told you I needed some time to think about things," he reminded me of something I already knew.

"Oh, so now I'm Ella?" I scoffed.

"What?"

I shrugged and threw my hands up indicating my lack of understanding. "I don't know. Two nights ago, I was Eleanor Page."

"Yeah. That's your name, isn't it?" he challenged.

Shaking my head, I sassed, "Not for you, it isn't. You've *never* called me Eleanor. It's always been 'Ella' or 'darling'. And if my memory serves me right, I can even recall a 'baby' once or twice in the throes of passion. But never Eleanor...until two nights ago."

"So, you've barely been able to look at me all day because I called you by your given name one time, and I didn't return your calls yesterday even though I told you I needed time alone to think?"

He was such a good liar. Because had I not seen what I saw last night I would have actually believed his inability to understand why I was so upset.

"Time alone? Really?" I sneered. "Max, at least have the decency to be honest with me."

"I am being honest with you," he growled. "Other than when I went over to Court's yesterday afternoon, I was home."

I rolled my eyes. "But you weren't alone," I murmured.

"Excuse me?"

I couldn't take it. I thought I was all cried out last night and this morning, but apparently, I was wrong. My eyes welled with tears as I rasped, "Did you call her 'darling' when you made love to her, too?"

Shock and horror came over him. Evidently, he didn't think I knew.

"Who? Ella, what are you talking about?"

He couldn't admit it? Fine. I'd tell him what I knew so he could stop denying it.

With tears rolling down my cheeks, I shared, "I was in my office last night when you got home. I saw you pull into your garage. I saw the other car pull up behind you. I watched as you stood at the back of your truck while she walked over to you." I paused a moment, trying to regain my composure. It didn't work, so I just did my best and kept going. "You hugged her, you followed her into your house, and ten minutes later, the light went on in your bedroom. That light never went off until more than an hour and a half later when she left, and you, presumably, went to sleep, never having returned my call."

Through my tears, I watched as realization dawned and Max's face got soft. His voice was gentle when he spoke. "Ella, darling, I did not do anything last night with that woman."

I didn't believe him.

And I wasn't going to allow him calling me 'darling' for the first time again since everything had happened affect my ability to stay strong for myself.

Max continued, "I get why you're upset now. What you saw, what you believe happened…your feelings right now based on your assumption are completely justified. But you're wrong. That was Vanessa. She is a long-time family friend and is a financial planner who took over her mother's client portfolio a few years ago. My father originally had Vanessa's mother handling his investment portfolio. Naturally, when I'd reached a point that I had money to invest, I did the same. But when Vanessa took over, I trusted the relationship we had with her mother to continue working with her."

Did he think I was stupid?

"And you expect me to believe that you discussed your investment portfolio with this family *friend* late last night in your bedroom?" I scowled.

"She was never in my bedroom," Max countered. "My safe is in the back of the master closet in the bedroom. I ran upstairs to get some papers out of it. I must have forgotten to turn off the light afterward."

Having been so convinced of what I believed Max had done and not wanting to look like a complete fool if what he was saying was the truth, I snapped, "Okay, fine. Let's assume you're telling me the truth about that. What happened to needing time alone? That wasn't what you needed, was it? It was just needing time away from me, right?"

"Not at all," he fumed. "And I've got to tell you, Ella, I'm really not liking the way this is going. You explained the reason for your attitude, and I got it. But when I tell you the truth about your incorrect assumptions, I don't appreciate having you insinuate that I've lied to you or that I don't give a shit about you, especially when you were the one who lied to me."

In all fairness, he had accepted the attitude I dished out, and didn't get defensive when I explained where it came from. Now, I realized I was being just a bit of a bitch by not extending the same courtesy to him. But I hated that he kept saying I lied to him.

Embarrassed, I kept my mouth shut and my eyes on him.

"I did need time to think," he started, his voice less harsh. "For crying out loud, my four-year-old niece was kidnapped. I thought that was the most devastating thing I'd ever go through in my life. But I was wrong. Because the worst part was when we realized she was being held for ransom and that we had almost no time to get a shit ton of money together that we didn't have readily available. Fuck, Ella, my niece could have been killed two days ago. And if it hadn't been for you, she very likely would have."

His voice. He was tormented by the idea of what could have happened to Claire.

"Max," I said softly, taking a step toward him. He took a step back, and I felt the sting of that in my belly.

He continued, "So, at the same time I'm trying to deal with what could happen to that little girl I adore more than anything, I learn that my woman is a billionaire. A billionaire, Ella. How the fuck does that not ever come up in conversation before then? How is it that we sat down to have dinner and a movie that we watched *on* your app, and you didn't think to mention it to me?"

I wanted to answer him, but I had a feeling he wasn't done.

"Yes, I needed some time to process everything that had happened. The biggest of those things being that if it hadn't been for the woman I fell in love with stepping up to the plate big time for my family and me, my niece might not be here drawing pictures of herself wearing purple dresses."

"You…you love me?" I asked meekly.

Shaking his head in disappointment, he bit out, "Christ, Ella. How can you not know that?"

My lips began to quiver.

"Instead of knowing deep down what we have between us, you sat here last night thinking that I was cheating on you?" he asked in disbelief.

A single tear leaked from my eye as I nodded.

He didn't say anything.

Then, I burst into tears and buried my face in my hands. Seconds later, I felt Max's arms around me as he pulled me close. "Darling…" Max trailed off. "I'm sorry about how I handled this whole situation. But you've got to know that I'm not that kind of guy, and I'd never do that to you."

Hearing that, I cried harder.

He kissed the top of my head as my hands left my face and slipped around his waist. We stayed like that a long time before I tipped my head back. I barely had the opportunity to do that when Max's mouth captured mine. We kissed for a long while before he picked me up and carried me out to the kitchen so we could make dinner together.

"I've got to ask you a question," Max blurted.

"Okay?"

We were cuddled up on the couch. He was on his

back; I was curled into his body. We'd just finished dinner and dessert a few minutes before, and while we ate, we didn't discuss anything that had happened in the last two days. I had a feeling that time was coming to an end.

"Can you tell me why you didn't tell me the truth about who you are?"

"Yes," I answered honestly. "It's the same reason I assumed you had moved on to someone else last night."

Max waited for an explanation.

"I thought that once I told you who I am, you'd leave."

"Why would I do that?" he wondered.

"It has been my experience that most men can't seem to handle the fact that I'm successful," I explained. "The more I got to know you, the more I liked you. And I didn't want to risk not having you in my life."

"Ella, I was eventually going to figure it out."

I shrugged. "I know. I guess I was hoping that if I could get you to fall in love with me first that it wouldn't be so easy to walk away from me. I really, really liked you, Max. I didn't want to lose that."

Max gave me a squeeze.

"Is it a problem for you?" I asked.

"What?"

After I lifted my head, I replied, "The fact that your girlfriend is a billionaire."

"Fuck no."

"Really? Not at all?" I pressed.

"Darling, I've got my own money. I don't have billions, but I'm not starving either. Any man who's threatened by your accomplishments isn't a man. Your ability to make a living and be successful shouldn't be stifled by anyone. And if a man loves you, he wouldn't want that for you either."

I couldn't help but smile at him. Max shot me one in return.

"Alright. So that's out of the way," he began. "Now we've got to talk about something else."

My body stiffened. "Why do I feel like this is going to be bad?"

"Relax," he urged. "It's not bad, but I want to explain why Vanessa was at my house last night."

I bit my lip, already feeling uneasy.

"Ella, stop worrying. I swear to you; my family has known hers for years. She really is just our financial advisor. After I brought you back here two nights ago, I tossed and turned beside you in bed. There were too many thoughts running through my mind. And it wasn't easy to settle down with you right beside me. So, I went home. It didn't get much better because I couldn't stop thinking about what you did. Fifty million dollars for my niece. I love knowing you feel that much love for me, darling. I really do. But that amount of money is not something I'm okay with you dishing out to ensure Claire's safe return. I had Vanessa come over last night so I could see what my options are for returning that money to you. King Enterprises has a high net worth, but a lot of that money is tied up in assets. I already have Vanessa working to move some of my personal investments around, so I can get you at least ten million within the next week or so. We'll get the rest sorted soon after that."

Suddenly, all I felt was bitter anger. I pushed up off Max's chest. "How dare you?" I chastised him.

Noting the drastic change in my mood, Max sat up. "Ella—"

"No," I cut him off. "You don't get to lecture me a few weeks ago about how I can't do something nice to thank you for the things you do for me and then tell me you want to return the money I used to get Claire back. That's the very definition of a hypocrite, Max."

"Fifty million dollars is a lot different than plowing a driveway or giving someone a warm place to stay for a few days," he reasoned.

"Maybe for other people, but not for me," I argued. "You just sat here and said you don't have a problem with me having money. Now, you're trying to take away the nice thing I did for you and your family. If I didn't want to give that money, I wouldn't have done it."

"If you don't let me do this, I'll never be able to tip the scales in my direction again, darling," he worried.

My shoulders dropped. He couldn't be serious.

"You can't possibly believe that's true," I tried consoling him.

"It absolutely is," he insisted.

"Max, they're already shifting," I shared.

He pulled his brows together in confusion.

"Did you see my refrigerator?" I asked. "Claire came here with a picture of her *family*, Max. I was in that picture standing next to you. She called me Auntie Nora. Do you know what that meant to me?" Tears formed in my eyes and my throat got tight.

Understanding dawned in Max's expression. Something clicked for him, and he took my hand and tugged me toward him. "Okay, Ella. I'm sorry. I didn't mean to upset you."

"I love you, Max. And the more I'm around your family, the more I feel for them. I adore Claire and Julian, and if I had to do it again, I wouldn't hesitate."

"It's not happening again."

My hand cupped the side of his face. As my thumb stroked back and forth, I promised, "No, it's not."

The silence stretched between us. When Max finally spoke, he asked, "Is that really all it takes for you?"

"What?"

"Plowing your driveway or pictures on the refrigerator," he clarified.

I grinned. "I mean, hearing her call me Auntie Nora was a pretty big deal. But hearing you call me darling is the best."

"Good to know."

I dropped my forehead to his shoulder.

"My house or yours tonight?" he asked.

"Mine," I answered. "I don't feel like going out."

With that, Max shifted me into his lap, slipped one arm under my knees and the other behind my back. "Ready for bed?" he asked.

"It's too early to sleep," I noted.

"Who said anything about sleeping?" Max teased.

I moaned as I leaned forward and kissed him.

When I pulled back just a touch, I breathed, "I love you, old man."

Max smiled against my lips and returned, "Love you, too, darling."

Then, Max kissed me again before he carried me upstairs.

Three weeks later

My eyes shifted from my computer to where the sound of my phone vibrating was coming from. I looked down at my phone's display, but I didn't recognize the number that was calling.

"Hello?" I answered.

"Hi, Eleanor?" a vaguely familiar male voice replied.

"Yes, who's this?"

"Eleanor, this is Agent Palmer."

My body went on alert. We hadn't heard anything new about Claire's ransom case. Max and his family reached out to the authorities a couple times since they'd gotten Claire back home safely, but they hadn't received any closure. Of course, they were all understandably on edge since the kidnappers hadn't officially been caught, and their family was specifically targeted. Jim had been doing some investigating of his own as well, but hadn't had any luck. The whole family had grave concerns about the possibility of it happening again.

"Agent Palmer, it's nice to hear from you. Is everything okay? Was there something else I could do to help with the investigation?" I asked.

"Actually, no," he replied. "You've already done more than enough. In fact, the reason I'm calling is to let you know that we managed to arrest all the suspects involved in Claire's kidnapping case."

That was such a relief to hear. "Are you serious? That's great news," I started. "I assume you've told her family, right?"

Agent Palmer let out a laugh and confirmed, "Yes, they are aware. Jim was the first person I called. I merely wanted to reach out to you and let you know that it was the information you provided to Agent Garza that day that ultimately helped us locate and apprehend everyone who was involved."

I let out a sigh. "I'm so relieved to hear this, Agent Palmer."

"Well, I'm hoping you'll be even more relieved if we're able to recover your funds and return them to you. It seems as though they transferred the money into a foreign bank account. Since we're dealing with international governments and banks, it's going to be a bit of a lengthier process. Regardless, I have no doubts these guys are going to be ordered to return the money, but you just never know how it's going to go. It might take some time, but my guess is it'll eventually come back to you."

"I appreciate that, but the money truly does not matter to me. I'm just thrilled that Claire is home safe and happy, and that you and your team managed to find these guys. As long as they can't ever do this again to another family, I'll be happy," I assured him.

There was a moment of silence before Agent Palmer stated, "Eleanor, I hope you don't think I'm being too forward, but I think it needs to be said. You deserve to know that Max King, Claire Golden, and their entire family are extremely lucky to have you in their lives. I've been doing this a long time, and there have been a lot of situations that didn't end nearly as well nor as quickly as Claire's did. And I've also witnessed some cases where people who had the ability to do something to ensure the safe return of a family member never stepped up to the plate. You should be proud of yourself."

Agent Palmer's words went right through to my heart. It meant a lot that he saw what I did for Max, Claire, and the family as a selfless act. I wasn't looking for any kind of praise, especially because my only concern was doing what I could to put a stop to Max's hurt. Even still, it was nice to hear that what I'd done was appreciated.

"That's very kind of you to say, Agent Palmer. I'm certain I'm just as lucky to have them in my life, too," I told him.

He hesitated before he agreed, "I have no doubt. Anyway, I'll let you go. I just wanted to give you the good news."

"Great. Thank you again."

"You're welcome."

With that, Agent Palmer and I disconnected our call.

I set my phone back down on my desk and took a minute to replay the conversation in my mind. When I did, the one thing that made me smile the most was that I knew Claire's family would finally be able to breathe and sleep a little easier at night.

EPILOGUE

Max
Nine months later

"**O**KAY. OKAY. I'M READY," ELLA DECLARED AS SHE hurried down the stairs.

I stood there watching her, not even remotely concerned that we were already late and were about to be even later. It was two days before Thanksgiving, and we'd been invited to go have dinner with Walt and Betty. They were important to Ella and me, and they both wanted to celebrate with us. Given that their kids were going to be visiting them on Thanksgiving Day and that we'd be spending that day with both of our families, the four of us decided that it'd be best to get together a couple days ahead of time.

Ella landed at the base of the stairs and was about to turn the corner to head in the opposite direction, when she stopped and looked up at me, puzzled.

"Are you ready?" she asked. "Why are you just standing there looking at me like that? We have to go!"

I felt my entire body relax at just the sight of her. She

was simply breathtaking, and I'd never felt so lucky in all my life. I tried to keep the tone of my voice neutral when I asked, "Ella, darling, would you please come here for a minute?"

She just barely dipped her chin before she started to move toward me. When she stopped in front of me, she wondered, "Is everything okay?"

My eyes roamed over her face. Every time I looked at her I wondered how it was possible that any other man that came before me was foolish enough to let her go. Not only was she incredibly beautiful, but she was hard-working, talented, sweet, and compassionate, too. What I liked most about her, though, was her sense of humor. Other than the one time after she told me about her financial situation and assumed I no longer wanted to be with her, we hadn't ever had an argument.

Being with Ella was just easy. And I believed a big reason for that was because we had similar values. Despite both of us having substantial amounts of money, we didn't need to be flashy. Ella wasn't materialistic. Sure, she had a beautiful home, but it wasn't loaded with things. The stuff that was important to her were lasting connections. Ones that resulted in pictures being hung on her refrigerator.

"Max?" Ella called, snapping me out of my thoughts.

"You look beautiful," I offered her a compliment.

She gave me a smile, pressed up on her toes, and kissed me. "Thank you. You look really good, too. I'm actually kind of happy that we're only going across the street because we'll get back here much faster."

"And then we can begin the real celebration," I stated.

"What celebration?" she wondered.

I cleared my throat as I took her hand in mine. "Did you know that when I walked up to your door before that storm hit, I never expected the door would open and show me the woman of my dreams?"

Ella's lips parted.

"But there you were," I added.

"Max," she rasped.

I went on, "From that moment I knew you were going to be someone special. As the days passed during that storm, I fell harder and harder for you. So much so that I began to dread the day you'd have to return to your house."

With tears forming in her eyes, she reminded me, "I was so upset about having to come back home, and you acted like it was no big deal."

Letting out a small laugh, I explained, "That's when I knew you were the one for me. I was trying to keep it cool. But the truth was that it felt good to know you were facing that day with just as much trepidation as I was. The thought of not going to bed with you beside me every night upset me."

I paused a moment to collect myself because I knew the next thing I said to her was going to send her reeling. "Then, the worst day of my life came when I got the phone call about Claire. And all I could think was that I needed you to be there with me. When we found out why she'd been taken, I thought we'd lose her forever.

But without batting an eyelash, you did what you did for a little girl you hadn't ever met. And that meant everything to me."

The tears were streaming down Ella's face. Even still, I continued, "I know you say that the scales are starting to tip in my favor, but I'm not sure they'll ever truly be there. It's not about the money you gave to save Claire either. I just mean that with the way you fill me up every day with your laughter and your spirit, I feel like I'll always be trying to fill you up the same, and I might not ever succeed. And yet, it's something I want to try to do for the rest of my life."

I slid my hand in my pocket, pulled out the ring, and dropped to one knee. Ella brought her opposite hand up to swipe at her tears.

Once I was on my knee, looking up at the woman of my dreams, I asked, "Ella, darling, will you be my wife?"

A sob escaped as she cried out, "Yes!"

I slid the ring on her finger before I stood up and kissed her.

"I love you so much," I shared, holding her close, her cheek pressed tight to my chest.

She gave me a squeeze and returned, *"Finally.* He's finally *my* old man."

I couldn't help but laugh. God, I loved her.

"It's beautiful," Betty declared. She looked up at me and approved, "You did good, Max. Congratulations!"

"Thanks, Betty."

"Ring or no ring, Max did good," Walt chimed in. He pointed at Ella and explained, "He managed to land that one. No better prize."

"Walt…" Ella trailed off.

"It's the truth, Eleanor," he insisted. "And let me just say I'm so glad this finally happened. Betty was driving me crazy from the minute you moved in across the street from us."

"I was not!" Betty scolded him.

Even though we both laughed at the banter between Walt and Betty, Ella repeated, "Crazy? I don't understand."

"The first time she saw you she insisted that with just one look at you, Max was going to be in love. But when you'd been here for more than a month and he hadn't even made an effort to introduce himself, Betty started losing her mind."

I looked to Betty. What she believed was the truth. One look at Ella and I think I knew somewhere deep down that she was the woman for me. But looking at Betty now, I was a bit concerned. She wasn't even attempting to hide the fact that she was disappointed with me. In fact, she was more than happy to share her disapproval. Shaking her head at me, she scolded me, "This town. The man you are. I couldn't believe you hadn't reached out to our new neighbor. So, I had to take matters into my own hands."

"Is that why you invited me over for dinner and casually put in that Max was going to be joining us?" Ella asked.

Betty reasoned, "*Somebody* had to do it! But then you got sick, and my plan went down the drain."

Ella started squirming in her seat. "Um, Betty?" she called.

"Yeah?" Betty answered.

"I kind of have a confession to make," Ella nervously shared.

Betty's eyes narrowed, and she didn't give Ella a chance to confess anything. She guessed, "You were never sick, were you?"

Ella shook her head. "Not in the medical sense. It was just that I had seen Max and thought he was amazing. I was entirely too nervous to meet him."

When her eyes came to mine, I added, "I'll verify this because when I finally did go over there, she was unable to speak to me."

Ella shrugged.

"Oh, what does it all matter now anyway?" Walt wondered. "They're together and getting married now. What does matter is that I've been smelling this food being prepared all day and I'm starving. When are we eating?"

Ella and I laughed. Betty gave him a chilling look.

Five minutes later, we sat down with the matchmakers around their dining room table so Walt wouldn't starve to death.

Later that night, Ella and I went home and celebrated.

It was the day after dinner with Walt and Betty. Ella's parents had flown in from Florida this morning and arrived only minutes ago. Ella had been bursting at the seams all morning in anticipation of their arrival. The second they walked through the door, she showed them the ring.

She and her mom, Vivian, had been gushing over the proposal while her father, Dean, looked on and listened. But he had something to say.

"Nori," her father said softly.

Ella immediately got emotional. I could see her struggling not to break down with just that one word from her father.

"I've been worried about you since the day you moved away from home," he began. "And even though I've always encouraged you to do anything you wanted because I know just how capable you are, you're still my baby. When I saw the news about the storm and then you called me asking about how long the propane in your tank would last, I had nightmares. I've never been so terrified in my life. I continued to worry even after you called from Max's place. It wasn't until a few months later when your mom and I finally got here and met him that I knew I could stop worrying like that. I have no doubts about this man and not only his willingness but also his ability to take care of you. I know you can take care of yourself, but I like knowing you've got someone who will step up to the plate when you need them to."

Ella threw her arms around her dad and hugged him.

I couldn't help but smile. It felt good to hear those words. I'd already known that Dean approved of us. When he and his wife came out months ago to visit, I found a private moment to talk with him. I shared my intentions with him, and he visibly let out a breath. It was like he'd been on edge for years waiting and hoping that his daughter would find someone who'd love her for all the right reasons. He gave me his full blessing to propose whenever I felt that we were ready to take that step.

Pulling out of her father's arms, Ella announced, "Okay, come in and get settled. We have a lot planned for the next couple of days, so this is the only day you get to rest and relax."

As Ella's parents walked farther into her house and past us, she turned and pressed up against me. She slid her arms up and around my shoulders with a big smile on her face.

"I finally get it, Max," she stated.

"What?"

"The imbalance," she clarified, which wasn't much of an explanation at all. "After Claire's situation, you felt like you'd never be able to even out the scales. You've got to know, I finally understand how you felt. Because right now, they're so far in your favor, I'm not sure I'll ever come close to balancing them."

"You'll figure something out," I assured her.

Then, I touched my lips to hers before we went in the next room to join her parents.

Want to see if Ella manages to Tip the Scales in her favor again? Download your FREE bonus scene here to find out!

www.authorakevans.com/tip-the-scales-bonus-scene

ACKNOWLEDGEMENTS

To my husband, Jeff—I was going to write a list thanking you for all the things you do for me, but I'd end up lengthening this book quite a bit if I did. So, I'll just say this…thank you. For everything. I know I'll always be trying to even out our scales. I love you.

To my boys, J&J—The love the two of you have for all things geography sparked our family road trips across this country we call home. So, I guess in a way it is the two of you that inspired this series. I can't wait to continue our journey across the U.S. and show you all that it has to offer. Not just the obvious, but all the hidden gems. I have no doubts you'll make it interesting. I love you.

To my loyal readers—From the bottom of my heart, thank you. I can't begin to tell you what it means to me that you pick up my books and read them. I hope this new series lives up to your expectations and that you'll continue the ride with me.

To S.H., S.B., & E.M.—It's easy to look at a book and see the author's name there on the final product, but it's the people like the three of you that really help it come together. Thank you for the work that you do to help polish my books and make them shine. I'm so grateful for the three of you.

To the bloggers—Thank you. This would be a heck of a lot harder without all of you. Your support means the world to me.

CONNECT WITH
A.K. EVANS

To stay connected with A.K. Evans and receive all the first looks at upcoming releases, latest news, or to simply follow along on her journey, be sure to add or follow her on social media. You can also get the scoop by signing up for the monthly newsletter, which includes a giveaway every month.

Newsletter: http://eepurl.com/dmeo6z

Website: www.authorakevans.com

Facebook: www.facebook.com/authorAKEvans

Facebook Reader Group: www.facebook.com/groups/1285069088272037

Instagram: www.instagram.com/authorakevans

Twitter: twitter.com/AuthorAKEvans

Goodreads Author Page: www.goodreads.com/user/show/64525877-a-k-evans

Subscribe on YouTube: http://bit.ly2w01yb7

Twitter: twitter.com/AuthorAKEvans

OTHER BOOKS BY
A.K. EVANS

The Everything Series
Everything I Need

Everything I Have

Everything I Want

Everything I Love

The Cunningham Security Series
Obsessed

Overcome

Desperate

Solitude

Burned

Unworthy

Surrender (Coming November 19, 2019)

Betrayed (Coming February 2020)

Revived (Coming June 2020)

Road Trip Romance
Tip the Scales

Play the Part (Coming December 2019)

One Wrong Turn (Coming early 2020)

ABOUT
A.K. EVANS

A.K. Evans is a married mother of two boys residing in a small town in northeastern Pennsylvania, where she graduated from Lafayette College in 2004 with two degrees (one in English and one in Economics & Business). Following a brief stint in the insurance and financial services industry, Evans realized the career was not for her and went on to manage her husband's performance automotive business. She even drove the shop's race cars! Looking for more personal fulfillment after eleven years in the automotive industry, Andrea decided to pursue her dream of becoming a writer.

While Andrea continues to help administratively with her husband's businesses, she spends most of her time writing and homeschooling her two boys. When she finds scraps of spare time, Evans enjoys reading, doing yoga, watching NY Rangers hockey, dancing, and vacationing with her family. Andrea, her husband, and her children are currently working on taking road trips to visit all 50 states (though, Alaska and Hawaii might require flights).

Made in the USA
Las Vegas, NV
06 August 2022